1

The Unforgiven

The Unforgiven

Robert R. Sytnick

Copyright 2021 Robert R. Sytnick

All rights reserved

IBSN:9798734220252

This book is the work of fiction. Names, characters, places and events are either the product of the author's imagination or are used fictitiously. Any resemblance to actual locales or persons, living or dead, or events, and times, is entirely coincidental.

Bobbyvr12@gmail.com

The Unforgiven

Chapter 1

High above the Shenandoah Valley, a lone raven takes flight, rising above the sparsely spaced sycamore trees, silently circling overhead. Its broad wingspan cuts the midday air effortlessly —casted shadows it leaves behind turn cold.

Drifting like a kite in the breeze, the raven glides smoothly, eventually landing on a branch of the sycamore. It peers between the rusty orange and yellowing leaves. Lifeless clumps of browning grass have lost their will and rustle with the occasional gusts of wind, adding eeriness to this desecrated ground.

Approaching intruders have interrupted the raven's slim pickings, found on the sand ridge of this desolate area of the Appalachian Mountains. Suspicious and intrigued, the raven vigilantly watches as a mystery begins to unfold.

* * *

The dust begins settling onto the dirt switchback trail that winds from the foothills up into the mountains. A reflection from the vehicle's circular mirror startles the raven—sending it into the skies once again.

The meshing of the reverse gear clunks into place, and the 1908 Model T backs onto the sand ridge that overlooks the Shenandoah Valley.

From a thousand feet above, the raven silently circles overhead, watching. A man wearing overalls opens the car door, puts on his brown hat and walks to his vehicle's trunk. He hesitates for a moment, and glances over the eerie area, listening, then removes a shovel from the trunk of the car. His large stature and unusual facial features brings the raven back to the branch of the sycamore tree out of curiosity.

A female passenger wearing a plain cotton dress and smoking a rolled cigarette joins him at the rear of the car. She points to a spot where he should dig, then calmly walks along the trail, lifts her dress and squats behind a tree.

After a short while, the man returns to the car without the shovel. The woman joins him, and they take a dismembered body from the trunk of the Model T. The body is that of a girl in her early teens. The twisting and turning while being carried breaks open the scabs on the girl's cut and disfigured body. Blood trickles onto the dirt, marking the gruesome trail. Her long blonde hair brushes along the sand, occasionally getting tangled in a twig, leaving small wisps of hair behind.

The pair mercilessly carry the body to a spot alongside the pre-dug grave. They set her limp, lifeless body on the piled sand. Her dress shows sections of blue fabric that was not stained with the blood that seeped from her.

The man and the woman casually walk back to the car, stopping and pointing to different areas on the ridge. The woman discards her cigarette while the man reaches in the trunk for a mason jar. Removing the lid, he takes a swig of the brew and passes the jar to the woman. She spits on the ground, wipes her mouth on the sleeve of her dress, and takes a gulp of moonshine, then another.

Without hesitation, the large man reaches into the trunk of the car, retrieving the young girl's dismembered arms. The woman sits on the edge of the car's rusted bumper, rolling a cigarette. She watches as he slips into the grave, then pulls the body in, turning the corpse face up and placing the arms next to the body. The young girl's cold, terrified eyes stare blindly as his chubby fingers close her eyelids for eternity.

Without remorse, he slowly covers the body with the piled sand, then packs the ground with his large boots and sprinkles a dusting of sand over his tracks with the shovel.

From nowhere, a gust of cold air suddenly twists downward from the top of the mountain, sending the man's cap rolling under a red willow bush. Covering his eyes with the sleeve of his shirt, he waits till the dusty twister passes. The female runs to the car and rolls up the passenger window.

Frustrated by the blowing dust, he rushes to get his hat. He trips, stumbling into a shallow sunken grave. Shaking himself off, he tramples and kicks the exposed rib cage, breaking the brittle bones like twigs with his big boot. Angrily, he heads to the car, cussing.

The gears grind into the forward position, and the car begins its trek down the mountain road. The raven, disturbed by what it has witnessed, returns to the slim pickings of the newly exposed rib cage.

No words, no prayers, nor any markers. Only the tears sent in the form of warm rain falling from the Heavens —onto the killing meadow that overlooks the Shenandoah Valley.

Chapter 2

To understand the hidden secrets of this haunting story, we must place ourselves in the times and footsteps of its people. Education was only a word. The Bible was just a book collecting dust under a bed. Moonshine remained a staple for existence, as did vengeance.

I am going to take you back, back in time, to where it all began and tell you a story of sexual appetites and a dreaded curse that haunts the people of the Appalachians to this day.

The vast Appalachian Mountain range has her soul resting across the state of Virginia. The Shenandoah Valley flows downward on the western side, covering the bleeding wounds of the Civil War when brothers took up arms against one another. The darkened past of that time still haunts the backwoods of this region. Echoes of the war remain vivid. Time has not forgiven the sins of its people, nor given up all the Valley's horrible dark secrets.

* * *

In the fall of 1851, Ebb Haggard's moonshine still was hidden along the bank of Dickson Creek, protected on three sides by Della's Gorge. Ebb lived alone, on his grandfather's homestead. His meagre income came from working at odd jobs in the county and the sale of his moonshine.

His stockpile of homebrew had grown as it did every season, and it was time to reduce his stock. Ebb hitched his mule, Sure-foot to a buckboard wagon and set out to neighbouring counties to peddle his shine. Every year Ebb stopped in Bridgestone County and visited the Evans brothers, who he'd fought alongside during the Indian Uprising. He had become close friends with Seymore and Clyde and shared the bed with their older sister Maude when he arrived every fall.

The moonshine flowed like the waters of Dickson Creek for a week. Ebb would eject his seed within Maude several times throughout his stay. In the one-room shack lit by a candle made from hog fat, the four shared more than moonshine— sharing the forbidden.

Their week of drunken sexual exploits left them hung-over but internally satisfied. Maude would gather a few personal belongings, joining Ebb as his quest went deeper into the county. He would sell his shine, and Maude sold herself. The joint venture was financially rewarding for the pair as well as pleasurable.

Tragedy reared from the past. In 1857 a jealous wife stabbed Maude in the stomach when she caught Maude servicing her husband. The woman claimed that Maude's trysts with her husband and her two sons the year before gave them a disease. She, in turn, had been infected by her husband. Her once plump body slowly reduced to a fraction of its former self.

Ebb and Sure-foot brought Maude's bloodied body home to her brothers' homestead for burial. In a fit of raging anger and grief, Clyde told Ebb never to enter Bridgestone County again, for tar and feathering awaited him if he did.

Ebb remained close to home for the next few years, carrying his rifle with him wherever he went, fearing revenge from

Clyde and Seymore. He continued brewing his shine within the confines of Della's Gorge. With local demand met, his stockpile of shine continued to grow.

In the fall of 1861, Ebb harnessed Sure-foot to the wagon and went to the vast Shenandoah Valley, then west to the Virginian border into Kentucky. He was in moonshine country. Within a week, he was able to sell most of his shine.

Sure-foot threw a horseshoe crossing Ripley Creek. Ebb walked the mule to the closest homestead. Old man McCluskey was a grumpy sort, meeting Ebb with a shotgun when the hounds alerted him that a stranger was near. McCluskey calmed down after a few swigs of shine and allowed Ebb to use his tools to shod Sure-foot.

Old McCluskey had done well for himself. He had two Clydesdale horses in the barn, four cows in the pasture, 20 acres of standing corn in the field, plus a pen of sows with young sucking weanlings.

Ebb knew a good thing when he saw it and eyed McCluskey's best prize of all, his daughter, Teress. Ebb stayed for dinner that evening, sipping shine with McCluskey and his wife, all the while admiring Teress. He was rather smitten with her, but she never gave him a second look.

Come morning, Ebb woke in the barn, having slept in the stall next to the Clydesdales. He shook the straw from his clothes, shooing the chickens away as he walked behind the barn to relieve himself.

Teress stood at the doorway of the house, calling out to Ebb while he harnessed Sure-foot. "You best come in and have a bite to eat before you leave."

"It's been a long time since I had a breakfast such as that. Thanks again, McCluskey," says Ebb, as McCluskey walks him to the buckboard.

"Aye, my Teress can do wonders with a frypan and hot stove."

"I see the corn is ready for harvest. You're going to need help to get it off before the weather changes," says Ebb.

"That I will. These old bones are having a hard time keeping up with the work in the field. Wilma and Teress do more than their share. We decided that this will be our last harvest. We are moving to Ashland come spring. Wilma has kin there."

"McCluskey, I was pondering and jawing with myself all night in the barn. Your daughter would make me a good wife in exchange for my labour in the fields till the corn crop is in your bin. My mule could pull your wagon to and from the field."

"I noticed last night at supper; you couldn't keep your eyes off her. You're rather smitten with my Teress. She is strong and has her wits about her, but she is somewhat on the plain side," says McCluskey.

"Yes, you're right, McCluskey. Her looks may be rather plain, but I could settle for a good woman like her who knows her place and will not wander."

"I promised her to the Kramer boy, Bubba, who lived with his folks in the next county," says McCluskey, pointing to the northern hillside. "The Kramer family and their kin joined us for Sunday services in the spring of this year. After the service, we gathered and broke bread together. Hank Kramer and I thought there was to be a wedding. Hot damned, were we fooled!" says McCluskey as he ponders.

"How were you and Kramer fooled?"

"That same day, after Bubba returned home, he ran off in the night. A week later, Hank sent word that his son never came back. I'm betting the young bugger ran off with Billy Bob Horton. Hmm, them two boys had a hankering for each other."

"Perhaps he is smarter than you thought," says Ebb, laughing.

* * *

Seventeen days later, Ebb and his new bride Teress crossed the Kentucky border entering Virginia. They passed through the scenic Shenandoah Valley with its cornfields picked clean. Cattle fed alongside hogs, grazing between the rows of harvested corn stalks. In the distance, small herds of deer roamed the fields, staying out of range of a rifle shot. Flocks of squawking crows jealously flew from field to field, nibbling on the sweetest fallen corn.

The sun began setting in the valley as Sure-foot pulled the wagon up into the mountains—leaving the contented sounds of thistles brushing against one another along the roadside.

The union between the couple was typical for the time, an arranged marriage where neither age nor means of livelihood mattered. Teress came with a dowry; two bred sows, a rooster and four laying hens. The endowment was significant in the lean year of 1861.

Ebb and Teress remained childless, as their marriage never was consummated. Ebb's fornication with women of the night and his love affair with moonshine had left him impotent. The shine now fulfilled his internal needs. Uncomfortable that he'd lost his manhood, he seldom joined Teress in bed. Her efforts under the covers with Ebb were fruitless.

Her oral manipulation of his lifeless penis aroused her begging body. Eventually, Teress found satisfaction within herself, but the craving for a man to enter her remained.

Chapter 3

Ebb Haggard kissed his wife Teress goodbye in the early morning hours of the 13th of March, 1862. It was a cloudy, damp morning as he walked into Singers Glenn carrying his trusted rifle. He joined the newly enlisted recruits that met in the village. Before dusk set in, the men paraded in the dirt street, then were led away to the military camp outside Charleston.

In the summer of that year, Ebb Haggard marched into battle wearing the Confederate army's grey uniform. Ebb was no stranger to the battlefield. He'd fought side by side with the men of the county during the 1849 Indian Uprising.

The bloody Civil war raged on. Two years had passed, word reached Teress that Ebb was shot dead at the Battle of Pikes Crossing. The Confederate Army had won the day and the fight, chasing the Union Army across the Delaware River. A sniper's bullet had taken Ebb down as Lincoln's Army retreated.

Teress was in her twenty-first year of life when she heard of her husband's death. Ebb would have turned fifty-seven if he had survived until the war's end. She remained faithful to Ebb, living in the backwoods holler, on the ground that Ebb's grandfather homesteaded. The entire farm was in disrepair, especially a small rotting barn that the westerly winds enjoyed picking on. Teress' pigs were housed next to the barn in a building where the corn was once stored.

Sure-foot occasionally used the rotting barn for shade and refuge to keep the flies off his back. The dilapidated farmyard was home for the mule that had aged with time and was of no value. Teress would chase and throw stones at him, keeping him away from the homestead in the event he died. She didn't want the mule's corpse lying near the buildings with no way to dispose of it. Sure-foot, the faithful old mule was left to fend for himself and pick his dying spot in the Appalachians—only the buzzards and coyotes attended his death.

It was four walking miles to Singers Glenn, a shantytown consisting of a few houses and a dry goods store. The village had no sidewalks or pavement, just the ruts left by the mule teams that harvested the hardwood trees for the Confederate Army.

Coil Parker was the preacher sent by the church in Charleston to bring religion back to the Singers Glenn region. The preacher ran off with Murphy's wife within two weeks of his first sermon. The two were discovered by Murphy when the Parson was blessing Viola Murphy's vagina on the oak pews while she held the Bible humming a hymn.

Murphy could not take the embarrassment and whispers behind his back. One cold night he walked, carrying a gallon of moonshine to the Tallawagga Bridge. His feet dangled over the edge of the bridge while drinking shine. Rolling a cigarette, he slipped off his shoes, letting them drop to the water below. The more he drank, the more internal disgrace he felt. In the early hours of the morning, he put a rope around his neck and jumped. The bridge is now referred to as Hangman's Bridge by the locals.

The local church was boarded up soon after the outbreak of war, as hostilities grew between choosing Lincoln's blue or Lee's grey. The church's once proud, stained-glass windows were shot out in 1861 by the Northern Army on a drunken patrol of the area. The only inhabitants of the church are the local nesting crows.

Behind the church lies the overgrown graveyard of Singers Glenn. At its entrance, there is a weathered wooden cross that leans to the east. Carved deep into its core, it bears the name of Hans Singer, who founded the village in 1721. The cemetery's population increases after every battle as fallen men from the village are brought home to their final resting spot. No cross bears the name of Ebb Haggard.

The schoolhouse had been vacant years before the Civil conflict. Guardians of the youth within the surrounding area did not feel the need for their children to read or write. Jedediah Smir used the old school to house his breeding boar. Most believed there was more going on in the old school than a breeding pen for the boar, but the fear to look outweighed the need to know.

Jedediah was the local entrepreneur of the village. He charged five cents for onlookers to watch his prize boar Jethro breed a sow. A mason jar of shine sold for ten cents, and a gallon reaped fifty cents, providing you supplied the empty jug.

It was the practice to place bets on the length of time it took to breed the sow in heat. Rumours circulated that once the boar did his duty and got penned up, the sow was fair game for men's pleasure, providing they had two bits in their overall pockets.

Teress Haggard called upon Jedediah twice a year to bring his boar, to impregnate her two sows. Her only income came from the piglets she sold and the few dozen eggs she managed to peddle in Singers Glenn.

Jedediah would leave the boar inside the pen with the two sows and return eight to ten days later to retrieve him. Hopefully, Jethro had dispensed his seed between the two sows.

Teress willingly prostituted herself to Jedediah in exchange for the boar's deeds. It was common knowledge what service she provided for him and others in the surrounding area. The local women shunned her, but privately she was praised by the sated men of the community.

In the fall of 1866, Jedediah returned with Cyrus, a Blue Ribbon, prize winning boar he'd purchased at the Harkin County Fair. He insisted that Cyrus remain with the sows for a week, giving him an excuse to revisit Teress' bed.

The youthful boar completed his task in short order. A few days later, as Teress watched Cyrus breed Sonia, the older of the two sows, she became stimulated by the young boar's sexual appetite. She sat with her back against the old barn wall, her dress slid partly up, servicing herself as she observed. The boar strutted his hard, coiled penis, which dripped with pre-cum as he walked around and around his conquest until the sow grunted once more. Cyrus mounted Sonia again and again. Teress watched intensely, moaning softly with pleasure as she came and came.

Two nights later, in the early morning hours, Teress hears squealing in the hog pen. She does not bother to get up, knowing Gertie is in heat. She smiles to herself, wishing that she had a night caller in her bed.

Chapter 4

Teress waves to Jedediah, seeing him in the distance coming down the lane. "Whoa, hold up," says Jedediah to his horse while backing the cart to the hog pen. "Teress, did Cyrus do his duty?"

"Yeah, he sure did. I watched him breed Sonia and heard Gertie squealing a few nights later. I see her tail remains curled. For the moment, she is a happy pig; you have a winner with that boar."

"Good, Teress. Cause I am feeling just as frisky. I'm going to put the horse in the paddock for the night. Oh, here, take this jug of shine to the cabin. I'll be along in a bit."

The two feasted on boiled pork, which had a few turnips thrown into the pot. Then they shared a wild raspberry pie and drank moonshine.

The single candle flickered as a breeze seeped through the poorly built cabin. Jedediah took off his boots and sat on the bed, waiting for Teress to pleasure him.

Teress approached him. She took the corn pipe from his mouth and stuffed it into his overalls. The flickering candlelight enhanced the moment as she dropped her dress to the floor. Her nipples quickly hardened when Jedediah ran his fingers over her vaginal area and around to her ass. He breathes in deeply, enjoying the bold aroma that radiates from her body.

"I want you to fuck me like Cyrus fucked old Sonia," whispers Teress as she gets onto the bed on all fours.

Jedediah, enthused at the opportunity, slips to his knees on the wooden floor, tossing his straw hat across the room. His hands caress her ass, his mouth waters and drools. Teress moans as his hungry tongue tastes her aching pussy. His fingers squeeze her hot ass cheeks—the scents and sounds are intoxicating. The craving for more is overwhelming as Jedediah's tongue licks her vaginal area up and down, swallowing every droplet she releases. Her hairy pussy tastes sweeter with every lick. Her fingers slide onto her clit as she massages herself. Instantly she cums, squirting a volley of hot fluid into his mouth. He swallows her magic and begins to suck her clean.

"Fuck my mouth, Jedediah, let me swallow you."

He anxiously climbs on top of Teress, teasing her lips with his cock while he strokes it. Small droplets of pre-cum greet her lips, her tongue licks the tip of his cock. He dangles his penis like tempting candy for Teress. One hand presses against the wall, and his other hand guides his erection into her mouth. Her hot lips surround and lock onto his penis, sucking while his strokes become faster and faster. Her hands grip his ass, pulling him deeper into her mouth. Suddenly Jedediah stops.

"I want to boar-fuck you."

Teress gets on all fours once again. Jedediah rubs his dripping cock over her ass. She backs in closer, and he inserts his penis deep into her pussy. With both feet planted on the floor, and his hands holding her hips tightly, he begins fucking her hard. The bed shakes while the sounds from them increase. The flicking candle loses its flame, along with its view. Teress cums, screaming out her joy as her fingers grip the blanket on the bed tighter. Jedediah begins moaning. He takes shorter strokes, releasing cum into Teress' pussy. Then pulls his cock out, shooting streams of semen onto her ass. Instinctively, he rubs the head of his cock in the cum between her ass cheeks.

* * *

Teress eagerly treated Jedediah to a night of passion in exchange for Cyrus's service. The moon was full that eerie fall night as the cold northern winds swept down the Appalachian Mountains, silencing the coyote's cries. Thunder roared, and lightning lit the night skies, guiding the falling rain to the ground. The one room shanty shook from the winds. Sexual appetites peaked, climaxing again and again, like the storm.

Weeks passed, and Teress realized that she was pregnant with Jedediah's seed. She tried hiding her stomach when she had to get supplies in Singers Glenn, but rumours spread quickly that Jedediah Smir was about to father a child out of wedlock.

Eva Smir could overlook the rumours of what went on in the schoolhouse. However, the gossip of her husband pleasuring himself with a local tramp did not sit well with her. Jedediah took up residence in the school with his boar. Occasionally he stayed with Teress when the urge needed fulfillment.

* * *

Dickson creek flowed red for a time in the spring of 1867, when Teress gave birth in the creek waters to her son, Beau. Word spread throughout the county that she'd given birth to a bastard son, and Jedediah Smir was the suspected father.

Teress' newborn son, Beau, was a comfort to her, giving her life quality and reason. She set the baby, along with seven dozen eggs in a wheelbarrow and made the four mile trek into Singers Glenn.

Word spread quickly that Teress and her bastard child were in the village. Avoided like the plague, she walked into the dry goods store cradling Beau in her arms. Redson, despite his wife's orders, took the seven dozen eggs on trade for household supplies. Teress expressed her thanks to Redson.

With her baby in her arms, Teress turned and began to leave the store. From nowhere, Eva Smir stepped in front of her and hurled a flask of acid across the left side of Teress' face. The acid quickly drips onto baby Beau's face. Teress drops to her knees. Eva Smir towers over her, screaming and threatening, "You bitch, you will bear the wrath of my curse. You and all you hold dear."

* * *

They say time heals, but Teress never healed. A mixture of guilt and hatred grew within her soul. She knew down deep inside that the curse would be her demise. The scars on her face had disfigured her once youthful glow. Now, she was looked upon as the county freak.

Beau, only 4 ½ months old at the time, was blinded in his right eye, and his top lip hung down over his bottom lip. To protect her child, Teress hid his face from everyone.

Eva Smir was never seen or heard from again. It's believed she had jumped or been pushed to the bottom of Whistler's Gorge, setting her curse into motion.

Jedediah Smir moved back into his house. He invited Teress to live with him in the village. She would have none of that, choosing to fend for herself.

Teress continued to prostitute herself to survive. Beau turned four years old in 1871 when Teress gave birth to a girl named

Edna. She credited Jedediah for fathering the child but knew that was only a guess.

Within months, the curse of Eva Smir struck again. Jedediah was found in the sow pen with his overalls pulled down below his knees. His stomach had been ripped apart and eaten through to his rib cage. The sow also devoured his penis and balls.

Jedediah Smir was buried without a casket on the dark side of Blue Ridge by the locals from Singers Glenn. The schoolhouse where evil had first taken root was burnt to the ground that Sunday morning—the Smir house mysteriously burned that evening.

Seasons changed like clockwork, and life was never the same in Singers Glenn again. The curse of Eva Smir hung over the village like the plague.

Teress had no choice but to continue selling her body to keep her children fed. Often her children would be in the adjacent bed while Teress pleasured her male visitors.

Chapter 5

The cold winds of change blew off the Appalachian Mountains in the late fall of 1884, blanketing the Shenandoah Valley in three feet of snow. With the winds of change, the curse of Eva Smir was quietly at work.

Wildlife would be scarce, and food supplies within the shanty depleted with a sudden lengthy storm. Teress sent Beau, now 17, to butcher a hog for food with his sister's help. Edna had sprouted like a corn stalk to Beau's height and was 13 years of age.

Beau and Edna were inseparable and often held hands when walking side by side. Their knowledge of the English language was limited, and the only contact they had with the outside world was their mother's callers. Teress feared the scorning of her children if they ventured into Singers Glenn.

The wrath of the unbroken curse would unhinge once again. Teress did not know that the curse of Eva Smir had struck quietly upon her family as the seeds of destruction grew.

Within a fortnight, the southerly winds from the Gulf of Mexico gathered, silting warm breezes over the Shenandoah Valley. The snow quickly melted, and the run-off over flowed the creeks and streams. The grasses flourished, as well as the wildlife. Nature was on course once again.

Beau and Edna flirted with life, perhaps on the wrong side of nature as they had seen their mother do so often. The natural order of right and wrong did not occur to them, for they never knew the difference.

Teress began having suspicions about her children. They would disappear into the woods for hours. When they returned, they were giddy, avoiding their chores.

One evening after supper, Teress follows them. She hides behind a bluff of oak trees watching Beau and Edna as they step on the flat rocks, crossing Dickson creek, then walk to the small open meadow. Here the grass grows above the dandelions, and the larks feast on worms.

Teress crosses the stream, hugging the tree line and hiding among an outcropping of rocks. To her horror, she watches Edna innocently take off her dress and lay on it, then spread her legs willingly. Without hesitation, Beau unbuckles his overalls, sliding them down and going to his knees. His right hand grips his growing erection, stroking it a few times, then sliding his penis into Edna's vagina.

Teress is furious at what she is witnessing. Tears flood from her as she sobs. Without thinking, she grabs the closest stone to her and runs to the pair. With her teeth clenched in anger, she hits Beau over the head with the rock. Beau slides off his sister, unconscious. Teress repeatedly pounds the rock against the skull of her son. Moments later, with the bloody stone in her hand, she realizes what she has done. She drops the bloodied stone —Beau is dead.

Edna, terrified by what her mother has done and fearing for her life, turns and runs naked, screaming across the meadow to the shanty house, not daring to look back.

Teress collapses among the dandelions holding her son close to her. Her emotions race, her pulse reaches new heights, and her thoughts run wild. Composing herself, she pulls up Beau's

26

overalls and buttons them, then lovingly combs his hair with her fingers. She kisses Beau's cheek, picks up Edna's dress and slowly walks home, stopping at the creek to wash her hands and face. Her reflection in the water stares up at her, and she knows Eva Smir's curse has manifested once again.

Entering the shanty, Teress finds Edna hiding under the bed in a fetal position, whimpering and chanting from the ordeal. She cradles Edna in her arms as the two cry together. Eventually, Edna falls asleep in her mother's arms.

Quietly slipping out of the cabin with a blanket under her arm, Teress takes the shovel leaning against the hog corral. She crosses Dickson creek and approaches the open meadow. With her fears growing, she begins walking slower, hearing every dandelion stock snap under her boots. The distant call of a curious mockingbird echoes in the meadow. Ghostly sounds of a stray coyote whimpering at the night sky cause her to stop momentarily. Teress begins to cry again as the horrific outcome of her actions now tears at her heart.

The purple moonlit night, glimmering downward to the Appalachians reveals the trampled path where Beau and Edna had walked back and forth on many occasions. Seeing Beau's body lying within steps of her, Teress stops, holding her chest with her left hand. Overcome with remorse, she drops to her knees. She combs through Beau's hair with her fingers, talking to him, sharing the many memorable moments they had together —choking on every tear.

Cruel reality quickly sets in. Teress knows what she must do. Wiping her eyes, she walks to the edge of the meadow, where the tree line begins. She pushes the shovel into the ground beneath a sycamore tree. She digs and digs without stopping, crying continually, asking God why He let this happen.

The first signs of daybreak begin peeking through the branches, and the morning dew drips off the soaked leaves. Mist filters into the meadow, sifting onto the grass and rising slowly as fog. The silhouettes of the distant tree line have become visible.

Teress throws the shovel from the grave and climbs out. Her body trembles from the cold and the task she completed. She wipes her blistered, bleeding hands in the wet grass. In a daze, she walks towards Beau's body. Her soul is empty, her mind has become blank, and her energy is nearly exhausted. Inch by inch, she drags Beau's body to the waiting grave. Wrapping his body in a grey blanket, she gets into the grave and pulls her son's body down. She kisses his cheek and climbs out of the grave.

Feeling someone is watching, Teress looks around. Edna runs out from behind a clump of willows, sliding into the grave with her dead brother. She lies on top of Beau's cold lifeless body, mumbling to him, hugging his unresponsive body as though she will never leave him. Her warm tears and saliva drip onto his face, almost giving Beau life.

The departing moon quickly hides its eyes behind the clouds in dismay, allowing the rising sun a glimpse into the open grave.

Chapter 6

With dawn's first light appearing over the mountains, a northern breeze swept down over the homestead. The ebony skies opened, releasing a continuous showering of light rain. Before the falling drizzle reached the ground, it turned into sleet.

For three long days and nights, Edna lay in the open grave, shielding her beloved brother from the forces of nature. The haunting curse of Eva Smir was at work. Like the storm, it seeped into the body and mind of this lost child.

Eventually, Edna's will to survive brings her back to the cabin. She falls to the floor by the cookstove, bewildered and exhausted. Teress quickly strips the wet clothing off her daughter, draping her naked body in blankets. She pours warm water in a basin, and with a rag soaked in red vinegar and salt, she washes Edna's face and chest. Filling the stomach lining from a butchered hog with hot water, she adds dried, crushed bat wings; to ward off evil spirits. Teress places the stomach liner under the blankets, firmly against Edna's chest.

Teress puts more wood in the stove, then dresses in her winter coat. She stops at the door; her emotions get the better of her. She breaks down, crying out loud. Her tears of sorrow splatter onto the wooden floor; she is lost, on the verge of a nervous breakdown. Her guilt is eating at her as she begins to hate herself. Teress sits by the table, wiping her eyes, and pours herself a cup of shine. Searching for the courage to go on, she takes another drink.

Staggering slightly from the moonshine, Teress carefully crosses on the stones at the creek, making her way into the open meadow. The northern wind retains its grip, and the sleet turns to wet snow, slowly melting as it covers the ground.

A lone raven, clinging to a branch tucked behind the trunk of a sycamore, watches Teress as she makes her way across the meadow.

Stopping a few feet before the piled dirt from the grave, she looks up into the turbulent sky, asking for forgiveness. In her heart, she realizes that she will not get an answer.

She grabs the shovel and looks into the grave, covering her mouth in shock. Beau is staring at her. His body is lying in six inches of cold water and melting snow. His once white skin has swollen, turning purple and blue. Beau's grey eyes have lost their pupils and turned completely white as if a ghost is hiding within him. The expression on his face is that of a lost soul, begging for freedom from the Hell he lays in.

Teress drops to her knees in prayer, sobbing into her coat. The falling snow melts on the back of her neck, sending a chill down her spine. She begins the gruesome task of burying her son. Her empty stomach burns from the moonshine, and her conscience eats at her. The strings that held her heart in place — break one by one.

As the last shovel full of dirt covers Beau's grave, the northern wind and the snow cease. The clouds move aside, allowing the sun to shine on the unmarked grave. Melting snow trickles off the crest of the grave, pooling at its base.

Teress crosses herself, mumbles a short prayer and begins to walk away with the shovel in her hand. She walks a short distance, stops, drops the shovel to the ground and runs back.

Desperately begging for forgiveness, she throws herself on the grave.

Night descends over the Appalachian Mountains. The moon hides behind the clouds, leaving a lonely eerie silhouette of itself. The light breeze mellows and is now hushed as it disappears in the darkness.

The lone raven that was watching from the sycamore tree takes flight, landing on Teress' back. It begins pecking at her neck, squawking, pulling at her hair with its beak.

"Fuck off, you bitch," screams Teress, flailing her arms wildly. "Leave me alone, Eva. Let this be the end of your curse," Teress yells as she jumps to her feet. Realizing she had fallen asleep, she hopes this was a bad dream.

Teress shakes the dirt off her clothing, picks up the shovel and makes her way to the creek. Sitting on a stone in Dickson Creek, she washes her face and hands. Blood from the blisters on her hands trickles into the stream. She spits on the blood blisters and rubs the spit into her hands.

Entering the cabin, Teress adds more wood to the stove. She places her hand on Edna's forehead, confirming that she is burning up with a fever. Teress gulps down a few mouthfuls of moonshine to warm herself, then heads outside to the root cellar for a large bulb of garlic. She smashes the garlic cloves with a rolling pin, puts them in a pot and places it on the stove. After heating the garlic and adding a quart of moonshine along with some crushed bat wings, she then brings the mixture to a slight boil.

Teress pours part of the brew into a cup, leaving the balance steaming on the stove for Edna to breathe in the vapour. Sitting on the bed, Teress puts Edna's head on her lap and then spoon-feeds the mixture to her daughter.

The shine Teress drank begins to relieve some of the guilt she feels, so she drinks until she passes out. When she wakes, she sips shine to clear the cobwebs from her mind. She spoons another cup of the potion into Edna, who is not responding.

Time has lost all meaning. The candles made of hog fat flicker through the night and into the day, burning freely. In the corner, at the foot of the bed, a spider spins its web. It glides down the rough board wall to the floor, feasting on dead flies and black ants.

The spider is confused and losing its instincts due to endless light in the cabin and the garlic-soaked air.

Chapter 7

A banging on the shanty door wakens Teress. She gulps a shot of shine from the cup as she stands, then coughs, making her way to the door.

"Orie Dodge, what the Hell do you want this time of the night?" asks Teress as she opens the door.

"Teress, I did tell you I would be back when Henshaw paid me. I have two dollars in my pocket and this jug of shine."

"Okay, Orie. Give me the money, and set the jug in the corner. You go to the creek and wash yourself up. You smell like an old hog. Now get."

"Do I have to Teress? Wash in that cold water, just for a bit of fun."

"You're drunker than an old skunk; you won't feel the cold water. You better get to it if you want lip service from me. Meet me at the barn."

"What's wrong with your bed?"

"I have a sick young'un. Now go to the creek and wash up."

Teress sticks the two dollars under a loose floorboard and sits by the table. From the tin of tobacco on the table, she rolls a cigarette and lights it. Inhaling the smoke deep into her lungs, she finds a moment of relaxation. Checking on Edna, Teress notices that she turned on her other side. She places her hand on Edna's forehead, then tucks another blanket around her, and spoons more of the garlic and moonshine potion into her daughter.

"It's about time you came along. I almost did myself, just thinking of you, Teress," says Orie. "Here, take a swig of shine from my jug."

Teress takes a drink from the jug and sets it down. Orie is leaning against the barn wall, massaging his penis through his overalls, waiting for servicing. She presses against his body, unbuckling the brass snaps that hold his overalls—the overalls drop below his knees. His hand goes onto her head, pulling her closer as she begins stroking his cock.

The more she strokes, the more his cock grows in strength. He moans as his penis is finally allowed in her mouth. Her hands grip Orie's ass as he begins to fuck her wet mouth. His cock begins to throb. She swallows every droplet of his pre-cum.

"Get on all fours. I want to taste you from behind," says Orie grinning with anticipation, holding his cock in his hand. Teress pulls up her dress and gets on her knees, revealing her ass to him.

She bends forward, placing one hand on the damp grass, spreading her legs to allow Orie access. He gently cradles her ass cheeks, rubbing them like he is holding a new jug of moonshine. His fingers tingle with delight. His eyes water as does his tongue, with the first taste of the pleasure of her wetness. Her knees find a new position on the ground and spread even further apart.

Teress leans forward, allowing the dew-covered grass to become her pillow. Her nipples harden. A craving guides her fingers as she romances her clit, while Orie swallows her precious flow of orgasmic desires. His hands squeeze her butt cheeks tighter, spreading them. His tongue and fantasy are out of control. He wildly licks and tastes all her forbidden fruit sending Teress into a state of bliss. She begins to release her sacred drops of cum, the deeper his tongue licks her vaginal area.

"More, Orie. I want more," says Teress, gasping as her body trembles internally, and she enters into a continuous cum.

Orie's hardened cock drips with pre-cum the more he revels in her delights, tasting all of her heavenly parts. His hand grasps his cock tightly, preventing it from shooting a stream of semen. Quickly, he thrusts his penis into her wet inviting pussy. Teress moans with delight, relishing Orie's throbbing cock deep inside her. He begins to fuck her harder and faster. His testicles swing in rhythm, slapping her clit with every deep stroke. Spontaneously, she cums again. Orie quickly extracts his penis, squeezing the head of his cock in his hand as it squirts volleys of sperm that drips from her ass onto her pussy.

He howls like a young coyote while spanking her ass with his cock, continuing to ejaculate sperm. Orie's fingers cannot resist temptation, and he rubs the cum between her butt cheeks and her hairy pussy. The fondling inspires new desires, and Teress' scent excites his sexual drive as his cock presses between her ass cheeks.

"Mama, Mama. Where are you? Where are you, Mama?" calls Edna in a weak crackly voice.

"Orie, get that pecker of yours away from my ass and back into your overalls. Edna is calling. You skedaddle."

"But, Teress. I want to spend the night with you. I gave you the two dollars and a half jug of shine."

"No, Orie. Edna needs me. Skedaddle. Go out the back way. I don't want her seeing you."

Orie pulls up his overalls and buckles them. He slaps Teress across her ass, "We have to do this again." He takes a drink from the jug and sneaks off into the woods. Teress struggles to stand, straightening her dress as she runs to Edna. "I'm here, Edna. Mama's here."

* * *

The moon, as does the sun, occasionally glances through the only window in the cabin, trying to catch a glimpse of the goings-on. Teress does not leave the cabin for days, remaining at Edna's side, nursing her back to health.

Late one night, when the moon is full, Edna walks past her mother as she sleeps at the table. She carefully closes the door to the cabin behind herself. Walking on the stones, crossing Dickson Creek, she follows the trail between the trees into the open meadow. Edna stands at the foot of Beau's grave and sobs.

From out of nowhere, the raven drops from the night skies onto the grave. It begins squawking, flapping its wings at Edna. She flails her arms at the raven, yelling and kicking dirt at the bird. The raven takes flight, circling over her into the darkness. Suddenly it dives at Edna, hitting her with its wing as it flies past her. It continues the attacks on her. Edna ignores the raven and lays on Beau's grave.

Teress wakens, wiping her bloodshot eyes with her hand. She notices that her daughter is gone and knows where Edna went. Pouring herself a cup of spirits to rid her body of the morning jitters, Teress remains at the table sipping from the container. She crudely rolls herself a cigarette, puffing on it, wondering how she can help Edna get over the death of her brother.

Chapter 8

Nightfall allows the agonizing days to slowly seep away and be covered over in darkness like a fitted blanket. In its quarter phase, the moon tilts in the sky, calling her tides home from the eastern continents. The warm Atlantic sea winds send banks of oppressive humidity, which shrouds the Appalachian Mountains by day, then turns into a ghostly fog by night. The sycamores stand side by side with the mighty oaks on the mountain absorbing the moist air. Their silvery yellow and rich golden orange leaves glisten with the sun's appearance. They twist and turn, chattering freely in the gentle breeze.

The calling of the seasons has sent the notorious beavers downstream into the Shenandoah Valley. Wolves shed their dark summer hair and are refitted by nature with a winter coat. Instinctively, they begin to run in packs by night, stalking their prey. Formations of geese cloud the skies, sending echoes of their calls throughout the valley. The lone raven finds comfort in the forest of sycamores—alone and watching.

Edna continues with her daily ritual, leaving the shanty when dawn first breaks, going to her brother's grave. She has lost her will to live. Her clothes are tattered and dirty. She rarely washes and eats very little when she returns home. Her body and her speech have deteriorated, and now she only mumbles, like an infant.

In frustration, Teress yells at Edna, forbidding her from returning to Beau's grave. Edna doesn't listen to her mother and regularly sneaks along the creek to the gravesite. Forcibly,

Teress binds Edna's hands with a rope during the night, tying her to the bed.

The next morning, Teress pulls Edna toward the creek. She struggles with her daughter, ripping the buttons off the front of Edna's ragged dress. Her breasts are exposed, free for the first time in months. A repulsive odour wafts from her body. In the struggle, Edna falls into the chilly water. Teress rips her soiled and tattered dress, throwing it to the creek's edge. Taking lye soap and a scrub brush, she scrubs and washes Edna. The foul water that rinses off her body flows downstream.

The cold creek waters continue flowing between the bluish-green and purple stones, carrying fallen rusty coloured leaves from the oaks. A white sticky fuzz that discharged from the cottonwood trees begins surrounding Teress' legs. She stands in the water in shock. Edna's freshly washed body reveals a hidden secret. She is pregnant. The curse of Eva Smir grows within her—like a cancer.

* * *

The cold winds of winter cruelly howled downward off the mountain, whistling through the evergreens like an unconducted orchestra. Dickson Creek lost its flow in January and froze over for the first time in years. The skies released nature's cleansing coat of snow onto Singers Glenn and the surrounding area. Each winter day became more stagnant and repetitive than the last.

Teress treks the four miles into town to peddle her eggs at Redson's dry goods store. She barters with Scagg Redson for household necessities. He favours Teress, often allowing her to get the better of him. She senses his sexual desire for her as his advances toward her cause him to stutter and blush until his wife enters the room to check on him. Teress knows and hopes that one day, Scagg Redson will be knocking on her door.

Edna has not visited Beau's grave in months. Her mind, along with her thoughts, have retreated as she slowly slips back to her childhood. She lies in bed, rubbing her growing stomach and giggling to herself. Edna's lack of appetite has slowly diminished her frail frame. Her teeth have loosened, and her hair begins to fall out. A once vibrant young girl has aged well beyond her years, but with the mind of a five-year-old.

Teress hung blankets from the cabin ceiling, preventing her male guests from gawking at her daughter. Winter was financially kind to Teress. The money beneath the floorboards has grown into a tidy sum, as well as her moonshine supply.

In the spring of 1885, the trickling waters of Dickson Creek run blood red once again. Edna leans against a rock with her dress pulled above her waist. Her legs are forcibly spread apart by her mother, who sits beside her in the stream of cold water. Blood spurts from her vaginal opening, instantly giving the creek waters a reddish hue.

Edna screams in terror and agony. Her hands flail in the air as she pulls clumps of hair from her head. Tears of pain, released from her eyes, flood over her face. Her nostrils run like the creek waters. She grabs a handful of pebbles from the creek bed, throwing them at her mother in desperation. Teress slaps Edna across the face, "Edna, push. Push, Edna. You have to push."

Teress slowly pulls Edna by the legs off the rock she was leaning against, immersing her in deeper water. The distraction confuses Edna and puts pressure on her stomach as she holds her head above the water. Edna's legs automatically spread, and her knees bend while digging her heels into the creek bottom. The blood continues to colour the waters while Teress' hand slips through Edna's vagina into the birth canal. The baby is in a breech position.

Frantically, Teress removes her hand and stands over her daughter, not knowing what to do. She knows God will not answer her prayers—or has He. For an instant, Teress' feelings are mixed and muddled. She realizes that her daughter could die, along with the unborn child. Is this God's will, she thinks to herself, or Eva Smir's curse?

"Eva, you bitch. This is all your doing. I hope you're burning in Hell," screams Teress as she runs to the shanty.

Moments later, she returns with the butcher knife and a pint jar of moonshine. "Edna, drink this. More, Edna, drink more," Teress yells loudly while holding her daughter's head up.

Edna gulps the shine from the pint while tears of pain flow into the open sealer. Teress takes the moonshine, and in one swallow, empties the jar. She lifts Edna's legs over her shoulders once more, reaching into the birth canal to turn the baby. The baby is stuck. Again, her hand goes up Edna's vaginal track. Blood streams out as Edna violently screams at her mother. Driven by the unbearable pain she is feeling, Edna grabs a rock from the creek bed. She smashes the stone against her mother's forehead.

Blood spurts from Teress' head, running down onto her face. Her eyes close. Her unconscious body floats like a rag doll down the creek.

Edna has turned on her side, hanging onto a rock in the middle of the stream.

"Mama. Mama," she screams. Her calls go unanswered —the bloody creek turns a brighter red.

Chapter 9

The raven, watching from a nearby oak branch, takes flight. It lands on the rock, which stopped Teress' body from drifting any further downstream. The raven hops off the rock onto her neck and begins pecking in her ear, flapping its wings simultaneously. Teress wakens, violently swinging her arms, sending the raven into flight once more. Her forehead is bleeding, and blood runs into her blurry eyes. Her ears ring with loud pulsing sounds. Splashing water on her face, she washes the blood from her eyes. On her hands and knees, she crawls toward Edna, who clings to the rock crying for her mother.

Finally, Teress reaches her daughter. She cradles her in her arms for a moment, then pulls her into shallow water. Teress spreads Edna's legs apart, then slips her dress up. Her fingers feel the baby's head— the baby has turned into position.

"Please, Edna. Push! Push hard. The baby is coming."

In seconds, the baby's head slips out of the birth canal, along with a stream of oozing blood. Teress holds the baby's head from falling in the water as Edna pushes. Her agonizing screams have silenced the surrounding forest. Only her echo bounces back; Enda is exhausted.

"One more push. Edna, push."

With that final push, the infant's body emerges from Edna's vagina. In tears, Teress cradles the baby boy in her arms. She reaches for the butcher knife that rests on a flat stone. Her hand trembles as she grasps the blade, slowly turning it, finding a comfortable grip. Her mind races, wondering if she is capable of the deed. Inside of her burning stomach and soul, she knows what she has to do. Gingerly, she severs the umbilical cord. The infant cries, gurgling out mucous. The child struggles for its first breaths, coughing and wheezing. Teress stands, holding the baby, and carries the infant to the edge of the creek. She sets the baby between two rocks in the thick grass, then returns to Edna.

"Edna, you did it. Good girl, you did it. Let me help you up."

Edna screams in agony once again. She is weak and terrified, almost unconscious. Tears pour from her eyes, and her nose expels a steady stream of mucus, which mixes with her tears and trickles into her mouth. Blood continues to seep from her body. She sets both hands over her vagina, trying to stop what is happening until her instincts kick in, and she pushes. Edna's strength, along with her will, fades away.

Once more, Teress drops to her knees on the stony creek bed. Her hand can feel another baby's head. "Oh, my God, Edna. It's twins. Push hard, Edna."

Edna does not respond to Teress. "Edna, push. Push, Edna." Teress' requests go unanswered. The vaginal bleeding stops. "Edna, Edna," screams Teress, but to no avail. Edna is dead.

Teress panics and runs to the baby at the edge of the creek, checking to see if it is breathing. Then she hurries back to Edna, standing over her in shock, trying to focus on what to do. Realizing her daughter is dead, she slips her hand past the baby's head, hoping to pull it from the birth canal. The unborn baby does not move or respond. Teress' heart pounds. She becomes jittery and hesitant, unsure of what to do next.

Suddenly she is knocked off balance. The raven has come from out of nowhere, striking her across the face with its wing. The cut on her forehead begins to bleed again, and blood drips into her eye. Furiously she grabs the butcher knife, swinging it at the raven as it swoops down at her once more. The vengeful bird lands on top of the oak tree, looking down at her, cawing.

Holding the butcher knife in her hand, she looks at Edna. Time is of the essence as the precious seconds tick by. She guides the blade with her hand next to the baby's head, slitting Edna's vaginal opening. Teress' empty stomach churns. She continuously spits until her body heaves, forcing her to vomit. Shaking her head to clear her watering eyes, she cuts deeper. Edna's blood and body begin to cool.

Teress sets the knife in the water and manages to wiggle her hand inside, pulling the infant to life. Turning the baby on its side, she firmly slaps the child across the backside. Again, she slaps its bottom. The baby kicks its feet, coughing and crying. Teress cuts the umbilical cord with the butcher knife. Gently, she sets the newborn girl on the grass, next to her brother.

Teress is in shock, hyperventilating as she stares at her dead daughter. She collapses on the grass alongside the twins and sobs. The newborn babies' cries go unanswered.

Chapter 10

The sun, staying true to its orbit, falls further into the western sky and slips below the horizon. A chill in the air now prevails as the day's breeze vanishes into the thickening air, awakening the sleeping fog. The serene sounds of Dickson Creek sending its once pure droplets of water down into the Shenandoah Valley calm the arriving dusk. The outlying forest becomes silent, perhaps in prayer —mourning what it has witnessed.

Teress' inner courage has regained strength as she approaches Edna. With a shaking hand, she closes her daughter's eyelids over the dried tears, which still clings to her face. Kneeling, she slides Edna's legs together and pulls her dress down, covering her. She places her arms around Edna's chest, dragging her from the rocky creek bed. Milk oozes from her breasts. The last of Edna's blood has trickled from her body, soaking into her dress. Teress stops, catching her breath while contemplating what to do next.

From the opposite side of the creek come the cries of the two infants. Teress panics. Her heart pounds with fear while she tries to focus. In desperation, she drags Edna's body through the thick grass, leaning her against a young oak tree. Making her way through the tall grass and crossing the creek in the dark, Teress kneels by the crying babies. Astonished that both survived the ordeal of their birth, she picks up the infants, speaking softly to them as she holds them tenderly.

Nightfall has set in. Reality sends quivering chills down Teress' spine as she holds the infants, knowing what she must do next. She wades in the waters, crossing the creek, carefully carrying the babies. Her arms have grown numb, and she gently sets the infants down in the tall grass. Teress sits and closes her eyes while pulling off a leech that attached itself to her leg. She places the bloodsucker on the navel of the baby girl. Finding another bloodsucker drawing blood from her, she puts the leech on the boy's navel.

"Are you listening, Eva Smir? Your curse will end when the leeches have drawn all the poison and bad blood from their bodies and fall to the ground," yells Teress to the night sky.

Without hesitation, Teress places the boy on Edna's chest. She slips Edna's nipple into the baby's mouth. The baby begins to nurse. The nurturing sounds calm Teress, easing her jitters, giving her confidence that she has done the right thing. The baby boy withdraws his lips from Edna's nipple and begins to cough. She knows the baby has drawn milk and needs burping. She picks up the girl and puts her to Edna's breast. Instinctively, the girl begins nursing as Teress burps the boy over her shoulder.

Gathering the babies in her arms, Teress walks toward the creek. She stops in the thick grass, crying, holding the two youngsters tight to her. She does not look back as she leaves her daughter's body behind.

Setting the infants on the bed, she wraps them in blankets, placing a pillow on each side of them. Her dry mouth craves a drink of moonshine, her soul craves peace, and her body craves sleep.

Teress rolls herself a few cigarettes, stuffing them in her pocket along with a pint of shine. Stepping toward the loose floorboard, she takes five dollars from her secret hiding spot. Walking on the northern road with a lantern, she stops for an occasional swig from the mason jar and a cigarette. The moon, which was shrouded over by the clouds, now begins to light the road. She looks to the heavens for a sign. A sense of being watched overcomes her. It is not the Heavens looking down at her, but the evil stare of the raven.

Two hours have passed, and Teress is met by three barking dogs crowding around her, looking for attention. Yelling and pushing the hounds away, she knocks on the door of a farmhouse. She knocks again. Through the crack at the bottom of the door, Teress can see a light.

"Who's there?" comes the squeaky voice of an elderly woman.

"It's Teress Haggart. Open the door, Mrs. Dodge," says Teress. She hears footsteps, then the unlatching of the door from the inside.
"Teress, what brings you out this late at night?"

"Where is your son, Orie? I need to speak to him."

"He's been working for old man Henshaw all week. What is it that you need him for?"

"Darn! I wish he were here. We, um, spoke a while back at Redson's Store. He promised to sell me a milking goat."

"At this hour? Orie, never said anything to me," says his mother. She looks into Teress' nervous eyes, smelling the moonshine from her breath. "Can you come another time? Perhaps in a few days when Orie is home."

"No. No, I can't come back another time. Orie said I could have a goat of my choosing for five dollars. Here, Mrs. Dodge, take the money. I am going to the barn and putting a rope on a milking goat," says Teress in a determined manner.

"Well, I don't know what to say. I wish Orie had told me that you made a deal with him. Take the goat, Teress. I will give Orie the money when he gets home. I'm sure he will go and see you if there is a problem," says Mrs. Dodge nervously.

The morning sun greets Teress as she ties the goat to a fence post inside the old hog pen. She latches the gate and makes her way to the cabin. The twins are still asleep on the bed, swaddled in blankets. Their fragile minds and bodies will soon need nourishment. The long walk with the goat has rid her of the desire for moonshine. She puffs on a cigarette while picking through the roaster of deer meat that is on the table.

Knowing this will be another long day, she must make the best of it. After rinsing a pail and wiping it clean with a rag, Teress makes her way into the old hog pen. She unties the goat and leads it to a clump of grass near the willow shrubs, then gets on her knees and begins to milk the goat. The goat relaxes while chewing on the fresh grass, releasing its precious milk. "You're a good goat. Hmm, you need a name. What about Nanny?" says Teress, smiling. "Geez, I hope Orie wasn't fooling around with you."

Walking into the cabin and setting the pail on the woodstove, she begins to warm the milk. She goes into her root cellar and comes back with the intestine from a butchered hog. Tying one end of the intestine in a knot, she uses a cup and pours the milk inside. The lining swells with the added liquid to the size of a small balloon. She lays the swollen intestine on the bed, piercing a tiny hole in it. "Come, little girl, you're first," says Teress as she places the infant's lips on the intestine. "There you go," chuckles Teress, as the baby begins sucking the milk that seeps out.

Soon the girl has her fill of milk, yawns and finds sleep. Teress does the same for the baby boy. "I am going to have to think of a name for both of you. Now you two, get back to sleep. I have to take care of a few things."

Chapter 11

Teress sits at the table, watching the twin babies sleeping. Her smile disappears as she ponders the task at hand. Pouring herself a cup of moonshine, she sips while rolling cigarettes. The shine that she sips gives her internal warmth and strength, but the courage to go on must come from the heart.

Her woozy mind wanders, thoughts of suicide encourage her to drink more. Hanging herself in the cabin is the option that seems the easiest for her. Life has been Hell since the curse of Eva Smir was placed on her. What of the twins? Should she put them in a basket along the roadside for someone to find and raise the babies? They will not have a chance at a normal life, inbred as they are. She knows the twins will be ridiculed and teased into a Hell of their own like Edna and Beau were. Suddenly, she yells out to the jug of shine that rests on the table, "Della's Gorge!" Her intoxicated thoughts are blurry, rolling through her mind—like clouds drifting over a darkened moon.

"Jumping off Della's Gorge with the babies would solve all my problems, and theirs also," she says to the silent jug of shine. Teress gulps down more liquor while fantasizing about her death. The cigarette that's stuck to her lip burns her, and she spits it to the wooden floor, cursing while crushing it with her boot. She stands, weaving from side to side. She stares at the sleeping twins, wondering if she should kill them as they sleep. Wiping the tears from her face, her hand fumbles on the table for her skinning knife. "Oh, Edna. What am I thinking?

I can't leave you out there by yourself. I will come out shortly."

Teress sits, clumsily striking a match on the table. She lights a cigarette, pours more liquor from the jug. Within a few minutes, the cigarette loses its smoke, falling to the floor. Teress' drowsy head soon comes to rest on the table. The candle made of hog fat burns through the night.

* * *

The morning dew has pooled together on the cabin roof. The warmth from the rising sun begins to release the captive droplets, sending them rolling down off the cedar shingles. The droplets silently fall in these bleak surroundings, past the window where Teress sleeps at the table. Their splatter to the ground is soundless within the tall grass that grows against the cabin.

The sun's rays find their mark, shining through the smoke covered window, lighting the room. Teress wakes. Nervously she looks around the room, hoping she was dreaming. Cold reality reveals a true view; the twin babies are sleeping on the bed. She quickly wipes her eyes. Reaching for the dipper in the water pail, she gulps water to quench her thirst and ease the burn in her stomach. She lights her half-smoked cigarette from the burning candle, then blows the candle out.

The guilt she bears gnaws at her conscience. Teress rolls three cigarettes, stuffing them into her pocket. She fills a quart sealer with water and leaves the cabin. Taking the shovel which leans against the shanty, she makes her way across the creek and up the bank. The wet dew clings to her boots and dress as she walks through the tall grass. Wiping the tears off her cheeks, she stands before the grave of her son. Grass and thistles have taken hold of the untended grave. The soil settled, leaving a dip in the centre. Teress cuts down the thistles with the shovel, throws them aside and smooths out the top of the grave. She takes a few sips of water, then sets the sealer down. Taking off her coat, she tearfully begins to dig a grave for Edna —next to Beau.

The sun begins to climb higher in the sky. Teress knows she has to get back to the cabin to feed the babies. Making her way back to the shanty, she stops and washes her aching hands in the creek. The reflecting waters are unkind to Teress as she stares at the image of an ageing woman. She starts to cry again, and the heavy tears plummet into the reflection, dispersing the image she sees. Wiping away the last of her tears, she sees the reflection of the raven looking down at her from an overhanging branch. Teress ignores the bird and makes her way back to the cabin.

The babies are hungry and crying when she walks into the room. She offers no comfort to them, only takes the pail off the corner of the cookstove and lights a fire.

Smoke rises from the chimney while Teress milks Nanny. She is not sure if her mind is playing tricks on her, but she thinks she caught a glimpse of someone knocking on the door of her cabin. Her mind races; could it be the law? Teress remains quiet, hiding alongside the goat in the tall grass.

"Teress. Teress, are you about?" calls a voice she does not recognize.

"Who goes there?" hollers Teress.

The man turns in the direction of the hog pen and begins to walk toward Teress. "It's me, Hank. I was passing by on my way from Singers Glenn. Well, you know. Hmm, I thought maybe we could have a bit of fun. I have money today."

"Golly, Hank. I have my hands full today. How about you come by in a few days."

"Are you sure, Teress? My pockets are jingling, and my urges are strong. How about just a quick one? What do you say, Teress?" grins Hank as he sways back and forth, showing off the bulge in his overalls.

"Naw! You best git. Come back another day. I'm too busy today," says Teress as she carries the pail of goat's milk past Hank and enters the cabin. Teress puts the container of goat's milk on the stove and heats it, checking it with her finger. She then pours the liquid into the hog intestine and feeds the loudest crying baby, the girl.

"Delilah. Yes, I will call you, Delilah. When my mother read the bible to me at bedtime, I was enchanted by Delilah in the story."

Teress puts Delilah back on the bed, picks up the boy and begins to nurse the baby with the intestine. "Now you, not sure what we will call you. You're a hungry little fella," Teress says, smiling. "I am going to take you and your sister down to the creek tomorrow and give the two of you a good washing."

Later in the afternoon, when Teress makes her way back to the grave, she started digging for Edna. Instead of a mason jar filled with water, she has moonshine. She quenches her thirst many times.

While digging in the grave, the dirt becomes loose on the east side, and she realizes she dug too close to Beau's grave. On her knees, she levels the bottom with her hand. Teress begins to climb out of the grave; her foot slips on the loose dirt. She hysterically screams as she falls back into the grave. She lays there, stunned by the fall. Beau's partially decomposed right hand lays exposed in the soft dirt.

In a panic, she crawls into the far corner of the grave. Traumatized, her body has released urine, and her dress is soaked. The ground she sits on has become wet, and she imagines the grave caving in on her. She passes out.

In the ensuing stillness, time takes its course. Teress opens her eyes. The raven is at the grave's edge staring down at her. Angrily she throws a handful of wet dirt at the bird. The raven flies to a nearby branch to perch and watch. Teress reaches toward Beau's hand and covers it with loose soil. Her shattered tears drop to the hallowed ground like falling rain. Memories of Beau and Edna rush through her mind.

The sun begins fading, casting shadows onto the meadow. Teress struggles to push a wheelbarrow with Edna's body in it. She stops several times to rest, talking to her dead daughter as if she is alive. With each bump, a foul odour exudes from the blanket which covers Edna.

When she reaches the gravesite, Teress drinks the last of the shine and lights a cigarette. She regains her nerve, sliding Edna's body into the grave, then tucks the blanket tightly around her daughter, leaving her left hand exposed. Teress begins to cry again— she places Edna's hand in Beau's.

Chapter 12

Darkness has slowly descended upon the Appalachian Mountains, chasing the rolling fog down into the valley. The moon refuses to look and hides in a maze of clouds. The westerly wind, which stirred the tall grass by day, halts. Whispering pines are silent this night, standing tall— guarding the unmarked graves.

After burying her daughter, Teress finds her way home in the dark. She quickly pours herself a cup of shine. Ignoring the babies' cries, she takes care of her personal needs first, changing into a cleaner dress and washing her face. Teress does not look into the small mirror that hangs next to the outdated calendar.

* * *

The forest comes alive once more as the sun rises, greeting the landscape and awakening the wildlife. The twins twist and turn in their blankets, crying loudly. Teress wakes at the table.

"Be quiet, you two. I have a headache as it is. Pooh! What is that smell in here? Y'all will get fed when I warm the milk," she says while putting kindling in the stove to start a fire.

The babies remain in their soiled blankets after being fed and fall asleep. Teress is carrying a bucket of water from the creek to fill the water trough for the goat. She puts the bucket down and begins to walk toward a man approaching her carrying a sack. "Orie. I thought it was you. Old man Henshaw gave you time off?"

"Yeah, he's been on my ass for the longest time to build that fence in the east meadow. I shouldn't complain. The old bugger pays good," says Orie.

"Bet you're on the way to Singers Glenn to spend your money."

"Yeah. Ma needs a few things from Redson's Store. She said you came over the other night and took one of my goats. What the devil do you need a milking goat for."

"It's kind of a long story, Orie. What's in the sack?"

"Well, um, a jug. Thought we would, you know."

"I know what you want. I can see that bulge in your overalls."

Teress takes the sack from Orie and sits on the grass. Orie joins her as they sip shine from the jug. Teress ignores his flirtations and sexual advances. He is growing agitated. His erection fades, as well as his urge, and he stands to leave.

"Orie. Orie, please don't leave. I need someone to talk to. You're the only person I can trust. Please don't go," pleads Teress as she begins crying.

Orie is dumbfounded and sits closer to Teress. He pulls a well-used handkerchief from the pocket of his overalls and wipes her cheeks. She takes the hankie from him and blows her nose in it, then reaches for the jug.

"What's the matter, Teress?"

"I don't know where to begin."

Orie puts his arm around Teress. She tells him about Beau and Edna having sex together. Breaking down, she confesses to Orie how angry she was when she caught them. How she kept hitting Beau with a rock, killing him. She goes on to say that she dug a grave in the back meadow and buried him.

There is a momentary pause. Orie rolls a cigarette and lights it, takes a few drags and passes it to Teress. She burst into tears as she draws the smoke into her lungs.

"I don't know what to say, Teress. Does anyone else know of this?"

"You are the only one I told. That damn bitch, Eva Smir. Her curse hangs over me like a noose. Bet she is in Hell —stoking the fires."

"Best you don't mention this story to anyone. You do not want the law coming around," says Orie.

Confiding in Orie has a calming effect on Teress. She composes herself and says, "I have to go check on the two young'uns. Give me a hand, Orie. I have to get them to the creek. They smell awful bad."

Orie carries the jug into the shanty and sets it on the table. Teress hands him two clean sheets. She puts Delilah in a basket, then takes the sleeping boy and places him next to his sister.

"You're right. Gosh, those two smell awful rank. Phooey! What were you feeding them?" asks Orie as he stumbles alongside her.

Teress sets the basket down along the edge of the creek. Turning her head as she unwraps the baby boy, she gags from the smell. Quickly throwing the blanket into the stream to soak, she begins to wash the baby. The fresh creek water abruptly wakens the baby, and he begins to cry. Orie sets the clean sheets down and backs away.

"Orie, come here. Look at this mark on his backside," says Teress as she holds the crying baby.

"Oh, my God! That brown spot covers half his ass. Look, there is another spot on his chest."

Teress wraps the baby in the clean sheet and sets him in the basket. The crying stops as he begins to drool, gurgling quietly. She unwraps Delilah in the same manner and immerses her in the water. Baby Delilah squeals loudly as the water awakens her suddenly.

"She has brown marks on her as well. Look how big it is, Orie. She looks as if she is wearing underwear. Oh, dear," says Teress as she wipes tears from her face.

Teress leaves the two infants sleeping in the basket. They are both wrapped in clean blankets and are being kept warm by the afternoon sunshine. She can see them from the open doorway as she has a few drinks with Orie. His advances begin to excite her, and her tense body is telling her she needs release. He puts his arms around her waist as she glances out the doorway.

She can feel Orie's cock stiffen as he presses his hips against her ass. Teress wiggles her butt to entice him further. He sighs as his wet lips nibble her neck and exposed shoulder. His hands slide up to her breasts, and he slowly caresses them. Her desires increase, and her body begs for more. His fingers feel like magic on her nipples— giving them a heartbeat of their own.

She can feel herself getting wet and turns toward Orie as he begins to unbuckle his overalls. Teress' eyes brighten as she takes his cock in her hand. Dropping to her knees, she strokes his throbbing penis. Pre-cum drips off the head of his cock into her hand. Without hesitation, she licks his liquid honey. The tickling of his warm pre-cum in her throat gives her an instant orgasm. She mellows, moaning, trying to catch her breath.

Orie places his hand on the back of Teress head, pulling her back to his cock as he strokes it. She opens her mouth and begins to suck his penis in a fast, rhythmic motion. Her hands anxiously grip his ass cheeks. Orie is in awe as his fingers weave in and out of Teress' hair. He quickly pulls his throbbing penis from her before he cums.

Teress knows what Ories likes. She gets on all fours on the wooden floor as he flips her dress onto her back. She spreads her legs, and his tongue savours the taste of her wetness. His mouth waters as it feeds on her moist vagina. His cock dangles in the air —like a willow branch, expelling droplets to the floor. The feel of her ass cheeks in his hands inspires his tongue to go deep inside Teress' pussy. She spontaneously cums again. His fingers play in her juices, and he begins rubbing them on her ass.

"Fuck me, Orie. Fuck me hard."

Quickly he rams his eager cock into her, and they move in unison until Orie thrusts his penis deeper, shooting volleys of sperm as he contentedly grunts.

Chapter 13

The afternoon sun peeks through the window reflecting off the empty jug of moonshine. The breeze which blew gently from the west is now hushed. An eeriness hangs in the air.

Suddenly, like the crack of a whip from the Devil himself, the sky rumbles, shaking the cabin— the gates of Hell have opened. In a rare occurrence that was only seen once before since time began, a scene from the Book of Revelations unfolds. An unexplainable phenomenon holds the mountains of Virginia in its merciless grip.

The sun's output immediately increases tenfold, sending its searing rays down onto the Appalachian Mountains. Terrified wildlife scamper for shade. Ground rodents find safety in their burrows. Fish swim to the lake's depths in search of colder water. Birds that took to the skies in fear plummet to the ground, helpless.

As a result of the intense heat, the air has lost vast amounts of oxygen. The twin babies awaken but cannot cry out. Their eyes sink into their foreheads. Their mouths open, gasping for air. The core temperature of the infants has risen to 108 degrees. They are internally on fire. Their brains cease to function.

Teress, struggling to catch her breath, tries desperately to crawl out the doorway to aid the twins but collapses. Orie is unconscious on the cabin floor, naked.

In a heartbeat, the skies instantly blacken. A scary silence prevails. Time stops momentarily as Earth reclaims its orbit. A total eclipse of the sun is in motion. The stars relight and find their shine in the ebony skies. The Great Southern Star, Athenia, which shone since the dawn of time —falls from the Heavens. It violently erupts in the southern hemisphere, creating hurricane force winds that rush in, feeding a blessing of oxygen onto the mountain.

The Appalachian Mountains lay numb, paralyzed in fear. Time re-sets and begins to struggle forward once more. The summer of 1885 will be like no other.

Teress awakens, gasping for air. Weakened, she forces herself to her knees. Her entire body becomes drenched in sweat. She begins to throw up. A ringing in her ears persists, and she has lost the ability to focus. She wipes her dribbling mouth and rubs her eyes, chasing away the sweat, regaining some of her vision. The basket holding the babies is in view, and she crawls to it on her hands and knees.

Orie stumbles out of the cabin; he is wobbly and shaken as he pulls up his overalls.

"Teress. Teress, are you all right?"

Teress ears are ringing, and she cannot hear Orie. She is slumped over the basket, crying and mumbling to herself. Orie slowly makes his way to Teress and the babies. He is dumb-founded and unsure of what to do. He kneels by her, putting his hands on her shoulders, pulling her away from the basket.

"Wait here, Teress. I am going to take the twins into the cabin. I'll come back to you."

Teress is oblivious to Orie's intentions. Her coordination and thinking capacity has left her, and she crawls behind him as he carries the basket. He sets the basket with the babies in it on the bed, then goes back to the doorway and picks up Teress in his arms. He lays her on the bed.

Grabbing a rag and the water bucket, he dips the rag in the water and gently wipes each baby's face with the cool cloth. Orie is disturbed by their condition and quickly removes the twins from the basket. He unwraps their bedding and immerses the girl into the bucket of water for a few seconds. Then sets her on the bed and does the same for the boy. Neither baby moves.

"Orie, are the babies alright?" frantically asks Teress. "Orie, are the babies alright?" she asks again.

Orie becomes quiet and stands. Walking to the table, he takes a drink from a cup with moonshine in it.

"I'm sorry, Teress. I think the babies are dead," softly says Orie.

Chapter 14

Teress lays on the bed feeling guilty, wiping her eyes with her hand, relieved that her nightmare may have ended. She gets up with the aid of Orie, looks at the twins and begins to cry once more— holding her chest as her heart sinks into her empty stomach. Their faces are burnt and disfigured, to the point where they are not recognizable to her. Teress drops to her knees, weeping.

"That fucking bitch! The damn curse of Eva Smir. I will never escape the curse's wrath."

Before Orie has a chance to console Teress, the raven lands on the window sill. It squawks frantically and loudly as though driven by an evil source. The raven pecks at the window in a rage, flailing its wings as though it is speaking to them.

Teress continues sobbing, her face buried in the blanket on the bed.
"Teress, look," says Orie, astonished at what he is seeing.

Miraculously the babies move. The boy coughs. The girl urinates on the bed as she begins to breathe. Teress looks at Orie. Her tear-filled eyes brighten. Her lips hesitate, a partial smile emerges.

Teress shakes the babies slightly, then turns them on their sides, massaging their backs. Their breathing stabilizes, and both infants begin crying.

"Orie, they're alive!"

"I could have sworn they were dead. Both breathless, I swear Teress."

"Can you go milk the goat for me? The babies will need feeding soon, and I don't want to leave them."

After a short time, Orie returns with the bucket of milk and places it on the stove to warm. "I found the goat tangled in the willows. The shaded bluff may have saved her. She was jittery, but I managed to get her up. She never gave much milk. I'm going back to tend to her"

"Wait, Orie. I don't want to be alone right now. That turn of events scared the Hell out of me. Somehow, I knew something bad was going to happen. Tell me what to do. I don't know what I should do about these two. Look at them; they're both disfigured and born into Eva's curse," says Teress, crying into her hands.

"They were conceived and born because of the curse. You know as well as I do that their souls belong to the Devil," sternly says Orie.

Impulsively, Teress slaps Orie across the face and begins pounding on his chest. "You son of a bitch, how dare you."

Orie grabs her arms, and Teress leans against him, crying on his shoulder. "I am sorry. I had no right to say that."

Orie steps back from her and goes to the table, pouring himself a cup of shine. Teress follows. She grabs a dirty cup, dumps its contents on the floor and pours herself a drink. They both sip moonshine without speaking to each other as the babies cry.

Finally, Orie says, "Damn it, Teress. You have to decide what to do. I'm going to water the goat, and then I'll go home to check on Ma. I will try to be back before sundown."

Teress feeds the children, and soon they are soundly asleep. She mutters to herself while pouring a drink as if she is talking to an old friend. Teress puffs on a cigarette. Her mind is in a constant stream of whirlwinds. She wants this to be over with, and killing the infants may be the only answer.

She sips at the shine, for it gives her the courage she needs. Her gut feelings tell her to take the infants and jump into Della's Gorge, thereby breaking the curse. She stands with the cigarette stuck to her lip, wobbling over to the babies. "Well, um, little boy. I best give you a name first."

She bends down and wipes a spot of dried milk from Delilah's lip. "You, poor little girl. Why did this have to happen?" Teress straightens herself and smothers the cigarette in her hand. "You're a tough little bugger. I'm going to name you Edsel. We may as well get this over with."
Teress puts the babies in the basket and sets it on the floor next to her chair. She gulps down a mouthful of courage and ponders awhile, then takes another sip as she rolls a cigarette.

* * *

"Wake up, Teress. Teress, wake up."

"Oh, Orie. Darn! I fell asleep. Uh, how's your Ma?"

"She's alright. Said the house got bright inside very quick and unbelievably hot. That's all she remembers. She woke on the floor, really thirsty with a pounding headache. Ma will be ok. One of my goats aborted, both kids and the mother died in the heat," says Orie, out of breath from the long walk. He sips from Teress' cup, then sets it down, "Where the Devil were you off to with the young'uns?"

"I was on my way to the gorge with the twins to end this. I can't take anymore," says Teress as she wipes the flows of tears from her cheeks.

"That's crazy! That's murder. They're innocent babies."

"What's the difference, Orie? I killed Beau. I may as well jump into the gorge with the twins— the Devil waits for me."

"You best think about this before you do anything foolish."

"Orie, look at them. They are cursed and now freaks of nature. Their faces are frightening. They don't have a hope in Hell in this life. Everyone will be pointing fingers at them as they did with Beau and Edna. Their only friends were each other. You know, in time, the two would be sleeping together, and I can't let that happen again."

"Yeah, I know. But murdering them," comments Orie as he picks up the jug and drinks from it. "Tell you what; ponder on it for another day."

Chapter 15

My Mother's family is related to Robert E. Lee, the south's great General, who led the Confederate forces during the Civil War conflict. When I was born, my mother named me Robert.

In the spring of 1894, my father, Arthur Billings, accepted an offer from the Virginia Lumber and Milling Company as their vice president. Leaving my mother Katherine, my younger sister Alice, and me in Richmond, he began work in Harrisonburg.

Dad is a great storyteller and returns every two weeks with adventure stories of the people and events in the Appalachian Mountains. Mom often twists his ear to quiet him, for the mysterious tales that he tells about the backwoods frighten her.

Mom insisted Alice and I complete our school term before the family moves to Harrisonburg. That summer, we packed our belongings and boarded the train for our new home.

I'm an excited nine year old and remain glued to the window seat, on this my first adventure. The steam train blows its lonesome whistle as it rounds each bend, and the feathery mist of the steam melts into the landscape. At times a distant echo rebounds against the window, captivating my mind as the train enters a series of tunnels. The sycamore and pine trees that grow along the train tracks seem to be waving to me. When I put my ear to the window, I can hear them whispering, tickling my spine with the secrets they tell.

I am enchanted! We enter a magical forest of pine trees and cascading waterfalls that cut their route down through the granite rocks for centuries. I stare out the train window, imagining myself as Robin Hood, leading my band of 'Merry Men' through Sherwood Forest. Gallantly I ride my trusted white horse with my bow and arrow quiver strapped to my back. My heart goes weak when I imagine my school teacher, Miss Clement, riding a sorrel horse, playing the part of Maid Marian. The sacks of silver and gold coins we robbed from King Richard's treasury; we return to the humble, overtaxed citizens.

* * *

The train slows and blows its whistle three times as we come closer to the village of Singers Glenn. Dad moves from across the aisle to join me on the bench seat. We both look out the window as the steam from the train blows onto the tracks, creating a mirage when we come to a stop.

"I was here a few weeks ago and managed to acquire the timber rights and leases to several wood lots for the Company. Crews will begin cutting this fall," says my father, as I continue staring out the window.

Suddenly, I feel a chill and reach for a sweater that is lying on the seat. The village consists of one short street running alongside the tracks and a few small houses on both sides. It is a sleepy village with little activity. At the General Store, a horse and buckboard are tied while waiting for a man to finish loading sacks into the wagon. Further down the muddy street, I can see an older man who limps as he walks, leading a brown cow and her calf toward the outskirts of the village. No children are playing in the street, nor do I notice a school. I feel sad and lonesome being here.

Dad moves back to the seat with my sister Alice and my mother. He sounds excited as he speaks, "Katherine, this is the area I was telling you about."

"Arthur, there is nothing here," says my mother hesitantly.

"I don't mean the village, Dear. The property we should purchase is a few miles to the west. It has a great view of the mountains and overlooks the Shenandoah Valley. There is a small lake stocked with trout. A perfect spot to build our summer cottage," says my father.

"Arthur, let's get settled in Harrisonburg before we make any decisions. When I look out the window, there is something about the village that makes me uncomfortable. Perhaps it's just me; you know I'm a city girl."

I press my nose against the window as the train blows its whistle leaving the station. My Robin Hood story fades from my thoughts, and I soon begin to fantasize about another adventure. Miss Clement is, of course, the leading lady in my story.

Chapter 16

Our family moves into a modest home within the city of Harrisonburg. Mom joined the church group once we were settled and comfortable in the neighbourhood. Alice and I never missed a single church service that year. Father was home every evening, except when he was working in the surrounding counties purchasing timber rights.

Alice and I enroll at the local school that fall. We both attend the same school, which is seven blocks from home. I promised our mother that I will walk Alice to her second grade classroom each day. Little did mom know that I had my fingers crossed behind my back when I agreed. Often, I run ahead and join my friends before class starts.

My fourth grade teacher, Mrs. Humphrey, is a large grumpy lady. She walks between the rows of desks carrying a yardstick in her hand and whacks it over your head if you don't pay attention. I quickly learn to pay attention in class. At recess, we sometimes make fun of a classmate who got a talking to from Mrs. Humphrey. When one receives a verbal scolding, she gets in your face and spits as she talks. I swear her breath can melt the chalk. Her breath is more punishment than the twenty lines one has to write on the blackboard.

I asked my father once if he would write to Miss Clement, asking her to move to Harrisonburg to be our teacher. He just chuckled when he told Mom what I said. I will never forget the look she gave me as I felt her silent reprimand. How was I to know that what I felt when I thought of Miss Clement was puppy love? I think it was more than puppy love.

The following summer, Dad gets his wish. He talks our mother into taking a carriage ride, along with Alice and me, to the property he plans to buy near Singers Glenn. Alice and I are excited to see where we will be spending part of our summers. Mom is rather pouty most of the day and even scolds Alice a few times on a young lady's proper etiquette.

We spend the night in Channel Rock at the inn. First thing after breakfast, with a basket of sandwiches, we are on our way once more.

The two sorrel horses pull the carriage with ease up the gently sloped mountainside. It seems like the birds came out to greet us this day as they flutter in the trees when we pass. Then the birds take flight into the sky, joining together as a pre-rehearsed congregation and swooping downward —like ribbons in the wind.

The tall pines sway in unison with each other in the gentle breeze while they shake the morning dew free. The mountains' granite walls are the silent keepers of this creation and peer skyward in the distance.

I shake mom's shoulder, pointing to the waterfall that I caught a glimpse of in the distance. Her right hand presses tightly against her chest, and I hear her sigh. She smiles, taking dad's hand as the carriage stops in front of a small lake.

"Arthur, this is breathtaking! I would never have dreamt a place of such beauty exists."

"This is a marvellous find, Katherine, and we own it," says my dad as he kisses mom on the cheek.

Mom and Dad are excited to be together in this, their secret oasis. They walk hand in hand like two school children. Mom takes off her shoes, lifts her dress and runs into the lake water to her knees, laughing. From a distance, I stand and watch them. I can see a rekindling of their love for one another. Somehow, at that moment, I feel different and begin to understand.

Alice and I walk along the edge of the sandy lake in the opposite direction of my parents. The sun is directly above us, and its reflection on the water instills a feeling of serenity. A pair of pinstriped ducks feeding on the reeds close to the shore gracefully swim towards the centre of the lake. We step over a few rotten trees, which the wind has laid to rest, and around the odd large boulder. Worms are poking their heads out of the moist ground, and frogs are hopping in front of us. Alice finally catches a frog and names it, Mr. Froggy. She insists that Mr. Froggy is going back to Harrisonburg with her, but I finally convince her it needs to stay here with its family of frogs —she sadly agrees.

Near the waterfall which feeds the small lake, I can see my mother and father wrapped in each other's arms. They are kissing. Icky, I think to myself. I don't know what to think, for I've never seen them showing so much affection for each other before.

Pretending that I'm not watching from the opposite shore, I continue on my way. Alice is playing with a stick she found and is pushing the lily pads further from the edge of the water. I lay on a flat rock that the sun is warming. The warmth of the stone feels nice, soothing my back, and my thoughts run away with me as I close my eyes.

I vaguely hear my mother's voice calling in the distance. I ignore the call and slip back to my dreams. My mind searches for where I was last in the dream, but to no avail. I can hear a snickering, then feel drops of water falling on my face. I wipe the droplets from my face and open my eyes to see Alice holding a soaked stick above me.

"You. I am going to get you for that," I say, chasing Alice as she runs toward our mother.

"Okay, that's enough. Children, come and sit on the lake's edge with your father and me. We are going to have a picnic lunch." said mom.

While we eat our sandwiches, Dad points to where he is going to build the summer cottage. He describes how the mill can cut the pine logs for the walls, and where the windows will be located for the best view of the lake and valley. With his finger, he draws in the sand the best place to build the boathouse and stable. Mom is excited as she places her finger over Dad's, guiding his hand to where she wants a stone walkway leading to the lake.

They share an intimate moment as Mom and Dad gaze at each other; neither speaks. Their eyes are locked on each other. Mom releases Dad's hand and rises to her feet. She looks a bit flushed; perhaps the pork sandwich didn't agree with her. Dad gets up and places the picnic basket in the carriage. He tells Alice and me, "The two of you run along and go play in that direction. Stay close to the lakeshore, but don't go in the water. Your mother and I are going for a walk. We will be leaving for home in half an hour."

I begin skipping stones across the lake. The water is like glass—each time I send the pebble further than the last. Alice is counting the ripples in the water as they glide to the shore. I place my hand on my forehead to block the sun from my eyes. I look again. Are my eyes deceiving me? I swear I saw a girl and a boy in coveralls in the distance, watching Alice and me. It scares me!

"Alice, let's go wait in the carriage."

* * *

Dad and Mom soon come into view as they slowly walk through the ferns and towering pines. They are holding hands and acting a bit silly. Dad helps Mom get into the carriage, and soon we are on the winding road. In a short time, we come to a crossroads. A sign reads, **'Singers Glenn 3 miles.'**

Dad tells us, "I will be in this area in a few weeks to acquire timber rights for the mill. There are a few farms that have nice stands of pine, which the Company wishes to lease. We could make a day of it and meet some of the locals since we all may be neighbours if we decide to build the cabin."

Slumped in the carriage seat, my mind retraces what I believe I saw. Shaking my head, I know I'd seen two children staring at us. There they were, a boy in overalls and a girl next to him in a dress. It feels creepy, like the way I felt when I mistakenly walked over Grandpa's grave during Grandma's funeral.

Chapter 17

It is two weeks later when Dad plans the trip to Singers Glenn. Mom is in charge of the church social that weekend and unable to join us. She made cold beef sandwiches with plenty of mustard for our lunch. I insisted that she make my favourite, peanut butter and her homemade strawberry jam sandwiches.

Carrying my young puppy Norman in my arms, he starts to urinate on my shirt as I take him to the carriage. Quickly I set the dog down on the sidewalk, where he continues to pee. Alice stands there laughing, pointing her finger as the dog's pee runs into a crack on the sidewalk. I go back to the house to change my shirt. When I return, Dad is crouched beside my dog, petting him, "You best leave him behind this trip. He needs some training before he rides in the carriage."

It is late in the afternoon when we return to Channel Rock. After dinner, I go directly to my room and fall asleep. Dad wakes us early for breakfast, and soon we are on the bumpy road again. Alice falls asleep with the morning sun warming her in the back of the carriage. I sit next to my father, holding a map of the area as he coaxes a team of young Percheron horses along.

Dad stops the team of horses on the road when a buckboard being pulled by a single brown horse approaches. The local farmer looks at my father's map, pointing out the route we should take. Dad shakes hands with the farmer and thanks him.

Eventually, we find our way to the Bonnet property. Dad tells us to stay in the carriage. He talks to a grumpy-looking man, holding a pitchfork at the barn door. I'm not sure what time it is, but I am getting hungry and reach into the basket for a peanut butter sandwich. Alice remains in the back of the carriage playing with one of her dolls. She is sissy talking to the doll as if it understands her. Glad I'm not a girl.

Dad comes back to the carriage with Mr. Bonnet, who is still carrying his pitchfork. I say, "Hello," but don't get a reply. He seems very eager to sign the timber contract and repeatedly asks Dad when he will get paid.

We continue on the narrow road, stopping at the Kenly's house, then the Hawker farm. Each time, Alice and I wait in the carriage. The yard sites we stop at all look alike, with a barn ready to fall over and a poorly built house. Paint is a luxury that no one can afford. The smoke which rises from the chimneys hangs in the air, perhaps suspended by boredom. The only colour visible on the weather-beaten buildings is the black tar that seeps from the chimneys.

Chickens squat on the windowsills, leaving their droppings behind. Grass grows in abundance around the shanty houses, covering the unwanted wastes. Livestock roams calmly and freely. The sun hides behind a passing cloud, and the breeze subsides. I feel lonely and bored waiting for Dad and climb in the back of the carriage with Alice.

Dad says he has one more stop before we go to Channel Rock for the night. The narrow road takes us alongside the train tracks into a village. I recognize Singers Glenn, recalling the village I'd seen from the train. Dad stops the team of horses at Redson's General Store. He pumps water into the trough, where he waters the horses and talks to them as they slurp the fresh water.

In the store, he asks for directions to Teress Haggard's farm. Dad allows Alice and me to pick what we want. I quickly point to the green, sugar-coated gummy sticks. Alice opted for the red gummy sticks. I am beginning to feel better as I stuff myself full of candy.

The horses are invigorated after being watered and trot down the winding trail. The landscape of the Shenandoah Valley comes into view when the path takes us to the edge of the mountain, then disappears once more as the road unfolds into the forest of pines. The air quickly cools as the tops of the pines shade the way, and the birds have vanished. An eeriness engulfs me, and I feel cold. The horses spook, sensing danger ahead, and rear up. Dad calms them with his voice as we turn into the Haggard farmyard. Again, he tells us we are to remain in the carriage. A poorly dressed woman comes out of the cabin and waits by the door. She wipes her nose on the sleeve of her dress and spits out her tobacco, saying, "State your business, Mister."

"I am Arthur Billings. I represent the Virginia Lumber and Milling Company. We may be interested in leasing some of your woodlands." Dad takes his briefcase and walks towards Teress Haggard. He sets the briefcase down in the tall grass and takes out a few sheets of paper. The two begin talking while pointing at the pines in the lower valley.

Startled, I duck as two stones suddenly bounce off the carriage.

"Edsel, Delilah. You too young'uns behave, or I will take my switch to you. Put down them stones," screams Teress Haggard at her two children. Alice and I are scared out of our wits as we peek out of the carriage.

"Are you children alright?" asks Dad. "I will be there shortly."

The sandy-haired boy dressed in a pair of overalls stares down at me. His face is dirty, his mouth is twisted sideways, and I can see small bubbles of saliva on his lips as he breathes. His breath smells the same as the horse droppings. One of his eyes points upward, in a different direction than where he is looking. The skin on one of his ears is brown. I think I just may have peed myself, feeling something warm running down my leg. I can't move, and I'm too scared to speak. My heart pounds as if it wants to leave my body.

The girl, wearing a flour sack dress, walks to the opposite side of the carriage and looks at Alice. She reaches in, touching the ribbon that's adorning Alice's soft brown hair.

"Hi," says Alice, with a friendly smile.

The red-headed girl doesn't speak and continues rubbing the ribbon between her fingers, awed by what she feels. She has an unpleasant look about her. Her thinning hair is tangled and knotted, revealing bald spots on her head. I swear, her eyes are colourless. They look in different directions and outglare the sun. The marks on her face are too large for freckles and trail downward onto her neck.

"My name is Alice," says my brave little sister, handing the girl a red gummy stick from the small paper bag. Instead, the red-headed girl grabs Alice's doll from her hand, backs away from the carriage, and runs into the bushes. The boy quickly follows her, stopping to throw the stone he has in his hand at me. Alice is bewildered as to why the girl took her doll and begins to cry.

Feeling the urine soaking into my pants, I quickly take my jacket, placing it over my lap to cover my embarrassing deed.

"Alice, what's wrong?" asks Dad, putting the briefcase on the seat and climbing into the carriage.

"The girl ran into the bush with Alice's doll," I say to father, pointing in the direction they went. "Dad, is there something the matter with them— they look weird and scared us."

"Alice, are you alright? Don't cry. Come and sit beside me. I promise to get you another doll when we get home," says Dad. "You have to remember, son, they don't get many visitors, nor is there a school for them to attend in Singers Glenn. The Civil War devastated Virginia and set it back a few generations."

Dad knows that Alice and I are upset. A few minutes after leaving the Haggard homestead, he turns to us and says, "We are only three miles from the cabin site. I have men working there on the foundation. Do you want to have a quick look or return to Channel Rock?"

I look at Alice, and she looks at me. We don't speak. Dad sees our facial expressions and turns on the road to Channel Rock. I go directly to my room at the inn, walking with my jacket in front of me. Locking the door, I rinse my pants in a basin of water, then wash the urine off my inner thighs and crawl under the covers without having any dinner. I feel ashamed of myself and want to go home and never come back.

Mom is in the garden with Norman when Dad stops the carriage on the street. She quickly comes to greet us. Norman nips at her heels as she walks. Alice is standing in the carriage, waiting for Mom to lift her out. She kisses Alice's cheek as she lowers her to the sidewalk.

"Arthur, how was the trip?" asks our Mom.

"It went well. I managed to get the timber rights the Company wants. I never had a chance to get to the cabin to see how the work is progressing."

"Oh well. You get washed up; I'll get lunch ready. Robert, take your dog for a run. He's been driving me crazy."

Chapter 18

The summer advances slowly. I spend a lot of time playing with Norman and training him to bark when he needs to do his business. As for fetching sticks, Norman has me trained for that.

Alice and I stay at Rebecca Hardie's place when our parents go to see how construction is progressing at the lake property. Dad knows that Alice and I are not interested in going. Rebecca and I are in the same class together, and somehow, she reminds me of Miss Clement. I don't think she wears perfume, but she sure smells good. Her father, Thomas Hardie, works with my father at the Virginia Lumber and Milling Company. The Hardie's house is on the same block as ours, on the corner where the gas streetlight is located.

During that summer, Mom accompanies Dad several times to our cottage near the lake. Each time they came back, the excitement radiates from their faces. Mom's plans for decorating the cabin and Dad's grand vision for the horse stable and boathouse monopolize the conversation at the dinner table. At times I wonder if these are my parents —how they seem to have changed.

Summer creeps into fall, leaving the golden leaves from the oak trees to float downward, covering the sidewalks. Red squirrels scurry up and down the naked trees, storing fallen acorns for the coming winter. The sounds of migrating geese echo from the skies each day. The residents are busy digging the last of the potatoes from their gardens. Storm windows are washed and added to keep the frigid winter winds out.

It is fun to be back at school playing with my friends once more. We all have our little secrets that we tell each other, promising not to repeat them to anyone else. I hold a secret deep inside of me, telling no one that I have a crush on Rebecca. Waiting for the bell to ring in the hallway at four o'clock is the best time of all because I will be walking Rebecca home. When no one is watching, I hold her hand as we cross the street. I never wash my hands until the next morning.

To this day, when I think back, the memory of her scent excites my mind, filling my heart with an indescribable desire. Then, the tears trail off my cheeks —and my mind repeatedly begs for just one more moment with her.

* * *

The sun remains faithful to its natural trek, slowly melting the winter away, sending the first signs of spring to the vibrant city. Subtle spring breezes gently warm the atmosphere. Clouds release rain once more, watering the plants in the window boxes and cleansing the city streets. The dormant oak trees have awakened to colour the neighbourhood with their share of greenery. Blossoms from the fruit trees send their fragrance into the spring air, recalling the insects from sleep. Returning dandelions take their place on the lawns, as do the push mowers.

School closes its doors for summer vacation. Dad previously promised me a new bicycle if I brought home a good report card. I pick out a Red Flyer bicycle from the Eaton's Catalogue that same night.

Norman seems to be gaining weight rapidly and begins walking slower. I leave him behind when I curiously venture down the street, hoping to find Rebecca playing outside.

Rebecca and I climb the apple tree, pretending we are pirates sailing on the high seas. Mostly we sit on the grass with our legs crossed, thinking of things to say. We inch over to each other on the lawn as we sit, purposely allowing our shoulders to touch. I can feel her heartbeat as I close my eyes and move closer to her.

In many ways, these are some of the very best times that we spend together.

* * *

"Mom, when is dinner going to be ready?" I ask, walking into the house after riding my bicycle. Mom and Dad are standing in the kitchen with sheepish grins on their faces. Oh, jeepers, I think to myself —they were kissing again.

"You best have a look at this," Dad says as he opens the door to my bedroom. Alice is on a blanket on the floor, petting Norman. My eyes widen.

"Perhaps you may want to change Norman's name to Norma," Dad chuckles.

* * *

Dad gets word that the finishing touches on the cabin and outbuilding are almost complete. Mom is excited. The furniture she'd purchased over the winter for the cabin is in storage in a warehouse. I insist that Dad invite Thomas Hardie and his wife Ada to join us at the cottage. He smiles at my request, patting me on the back.

Our two families board the train a week later. Norma is placed in a wire crate and rides in the baggage car with her two pups. I haven't yet given the puppies each a name. They appear identical, all white with a brown patch over their left eye. I just call both of them Spot, for now. Once they are older, I know each will take on a unique personality of their own, and the appropriate name will suddenly come to light.

Rebecca and I share a seat on the train. Our breath clings to the glass of the window as we look out at the mysterious rock formations towering in the background. Some of the rocks resemble people, and we give them names. I look around before printing Rebecca's name on the steamy glass. She giggles into her hand as I add a heart shape around her name. Feeling shy, I wipe the window clean with the sleeve of my jacket. My warm breath on the window soon fogs it up again, and we play Xs & Os on the glass.

The train whistle sounds three times as it rounds the bend, coming to a stop in Singers Glenn. Two carriages are waiting for us, and each family gets into a carriage. People are gathered around Redson's General Store. Dad asks the carriage driver what is going on. "Old lady Redson died. She fell dead to the floor while stocking shelves," says the driver.

When we arrive at the cabin, the delivery men from Harrisonburg are unloading the furniture from a wagon and carrying it into the house. Mom quickly gets out of the carriage, telling the men where to place everything. Dad, along with Mr. Hardie, helps bring the icebox into the cabin. Rebecca joins me as we run along the lakeshore with Norma and the pups following us. We skip stones on the water, trying to entice the Spots to chase the pebbles we throw. Eventually, Alice comes along carrying her doll and interrupts our fun.

"Robert, Mom said that you are to look out for me."

Mom is in her glory over the furniture she had chosen for the cabin. Ada helps Mom cook our first dinner at the cabin with friends. I make a point of sitting next to Rebecca at the table.

In the morning, I can hear Dad and Thomas fumbling in the kitchen. Soon the smell of coffee brewing radiates through the cabin, and I wipe the Sandman's blessing from my eyes. Dad and Thomas head to the boathouse and slip the boat into the lake waters. Rebecca and I watch them fish from a distance as we play with the pups on the sandy shore. I am apprehensive about venturing too far from the cabin. An uneasy feeling persists in haunting me, and I continually look toward the opposite shore. Somehow, I know that someone is watching us.

A few days later, Dad and Thomas hitch the team of horses to the carriage. The weather has turned. Clouds begin releasing light rain, causing the fog to rise from the lake. I help Dad pull the top over the carriage and join him in the front seat. Mr. and Mrs. Hardie ride in the back with Rebecca as we make our way to the train station in Singers Glenn. We wave goodbye when the train pulls away from the station. I feel a sense of emptiness, watching Rebecca leaving with her parents.

Dad stops the carriage at Redson's store, and I follow him in, hoping to get some candy. Scagg Redson hands me a small paper bag of gummy sticks. "Is it the red ones your sister likes?" asks Dad.

I stuff the paper bag of gummy sticks into my jacket pocket and look around the store, munching on a piece of the candy. Dad stands next to the counter, offering his condolences to Scagg, apologizing for not attending his wife's funeral. I hear the horses whinny and look out the window. It's them! It's the boy and girl who took Alice's doll. They are holding hands as they slip from behind a building across the street and walk bravely into Redson's store, not recognizing my Dad or me.

"I will be with the two of you in a moment. Stay where you are," says Redson, as he excuses himself from Dad.

Neither of them moves or speaks until the girl steps forward, pointing to a tin of Chum tobacco on the shelf behind the counter. She walks a few feet, stops at the bags of flour, touches a sack, and then tries to speak but only mumbles. The boy merely stands in the aisle playing with his jackknife, grinning to himself.

"Dad. Dad, they're the ones that took Alice's doll," I say, running to his side.

The girl is startled and squats like she is going to pee herself. The boy stares into my eyes without a word. He purposely closes the blade on his jackknife slowly while glaring at me. They both run from the store, stop on the dirt street and look for stones to throw. Redson runs out the door, yelling at them. The words are swear words I never heard before.

The glare Edsel gave me that summer afternoon in Redson's store sinks deep into my stomach, sending chills to my hollow core. I know I was in the presence of evil —his piercing gaze remains vivid in my mind to this day.

Chapter 19

Lightning crackles in the distance, and the skies open, releasing short bursts of heavy rain. Daylight quickly vanishes within the darkening turbulence, and thunder echoes from the mountain top. A cold chill sweeps along the muddy street and clings to everything in its path.

I zip up my jacket and stand under the awning of Redson's store, looking to see if the two Haggard kids are watching. Without notice, the rain suddenly stops as if a curtain is drawn over the village. The sun begins to shine, banishing the clouds from the sky. The horses raise their heads, shaking the rain from their coats. A cat crawls out from under the store's steps and gingerly makes its way around the puddled water as it crosses the street.

I keep my distance from Scagg and Dad, sitting on a 50 pound barrel of four inch nails, listening to Scagg tell my father the story of Eva Smir's curse. Dad is intrigued by Redson's words and barely moves a muscle as he listens. Scagg continues, telling Dad about Beau and Edna and their mysterious disappearance.

"There were rumours that Beau ran off and joined the army. Some say he jumped off Della's gorge because people teased him wherever he went. Believe me, Arthur, he was not pleasant to look at," quietly says Scagg.

"What about Edna?" curiously asks Dad.

"Once, when I delivered an order of groceries to her place, I asked Teress where Edna is." All she said is that Edna went to help her kin in Ashland."

"Who fathered the two that were here in the store?" asks Dad.

Redson's face turns red. He steps back from the counter, somewhat flustered, pondering what to say. Dad knows he has struck a nerve. I turn my head, pretending not to be listening and pull another gummy stick from the paper bag.

"I never dared to ask Teress. Somehow that damn curse played a big role in her life and everyone who comes into contact with her. Rumours abound that Delilah and Edsel are the offspring of one of Teress' male visitors. Another theory is that Edna also prostituted herself, getting pregnant with the twins. To my way of thinking, Edsel and Delilah appear to be inbred. I believe Edna's brother Beau was the father," quietly says Scagg. He then shakes his head—not wanting to believe what he just said.

"Fascinating, yet very disturbing," says Dad as he buttons his jacket. "Robert, shall we get back to the cabin? Your mother and Alice must be wondering what is keeping us."

Dad is not his usual self on the way to the cottage. He seems to be deep in thought. His habit of talking to the horses as they pull the carriage is missing this afternoon, and the horses sense it. Somehow, I get the feeling that a fear has attached itself to my Dad, after hearing Scagg's story.

Alice comes out to greet us. Norma and the pups follow her. She asks Dad if he has any gummy sticks for her. Unexpectedly, he picks Alice up and hugs her, carrying her into the cabin. I tie the horses to the cross rail beside the stables and go to see what Mom is doing. Dad is embracing Mom while they stand at the counter in the kitchen. One of the pups is jealously growling as it tugs on the cuff of Dad's trousers.

* * *

The rain starts falling again later that evening and continues into the next morning. By late afternoon, the sun finds its way from between the clouds and shines on the lake. I run along the water's edge, and the pups follow me, barking and nipping at each other's ears. When I stop, one of the puppies runs into me and tumbles onto the sand. The other pup pounces on it, and the small skirmish is on, causing me to laugh. Norma follows us. Occasionally, she stops and stares across the lake. Her ears perk up, and she murmurs something short of a growl. Somehow, I feel she is uncomfortable and edgy when we are here at the lake.

Alice is sitting on the grass near the cabin, playing with those silly dolls of hers. Dad and Mom are in the cabin. Once in a while, when I look back, I can see the curtain moving. They are keeping an eye on us, and I think they are doing that kissing stuff again.

After supper, we sit around the fireplace. Mom is knitting, and of course, Alice is talking to her dolls. I'm in the entranceway playing with the pups when Dad says, "We will be heading back to Harrisonburg the day after tomorrow. School starts soon for the two of you, so let's make the best of tomorrow. I thought we could all go fishing on the lake. What do you say?"

* * *

The morning has left its blessing of dew on the cabin. From my bedroom window, I watch as droplets fall from the shingles. There is no sound, only a lonely silence. The sun has awakened in the east and is beginning to attempt its climb into the sky. The narrow horizon has streaks of golden oranges and yellows, trying to smother out the majestic blues and purples that hold the night tightly together. A silhouette of the majestic pine trees cast a shadow in the background, hiding the mountains from view.

Glitter on the lake fascinates my mind as I imagine a mirage of dancing ghosts performing for the Heavens above. The dance group swoops from one end of the lake to the other with magical ease. A prism of colours beams off and through the performers, slowly vanishing into the morning sun, warming my thoughts. In those few moments, I feel lonely and empty. Something stirs inside of me— I realize how much I miss Rebecca.

Dad has his trousers rolled up to his knees as he pushes the boat into the water. He quickly climbs in as Mom and I paddle the boat from the shore. His socks were left on the shore, only to be found by the pups who play tug-of-war with them. Norma pays no attention to the puppies as she sits on her hindquarters, watching us paddle to the centre of the lake.

Dad puts a worm onto the hook of Mom's fishing line while I loop kernels of corn onto my hook, sending it to the bottom of the lake. Alice is not at all interested in fishing. She is in a world of her own, playing with her doll.

The sun finds its strength in the early afternoon. Mom anticipated that we would not catch any fish and packed a lunch. So much for Dad's plans for a fish fry.

Norma is acting strange. She keeps walking toward a clump of shrubs, barking and then running back to her pups. She must be after a squirrel or groundhog, I think.

Suddenly, I feel a tug on my line. My heart skips a beat, my first fish. "Dad, Dad! What do I do?"

"Jerk your line so the hook sets in the fish's mouth. Son, reel the fish to the boat," says Dad excitedly.

Oh geez, I need to pee. My mind runs away with me as I reel the fish toward the boat, thinking to myself, I hope it's a big fish. I pay no attention to Norma's barking; my priority is getting my first fish into the boat.

Dad moves closer to me. "I will net the fish when it comes to the surface. Keep reeling it in, don't give it any slack." Dad anxiously swoops the net into the water and raises it above the boat for all of us to see my catch.

"An old boot filled with water," I sadly say. "Damn it! I thought I had a fish, not some kid's boot."

Mom chuckles into her hand, and Dad rubs my head. Alice is oblivious to what is happening as she combs her doll's hair.

"Where did Norma go? The pups are gone. Dad, let's get back to the shore. I can hear her barking at something."

I help my Dad row the boat. My arms ache, but I ignore the pain as I keep looking toward the shore. Finally, I can feel the bottom of the boat skim onto the sand at the shore. Dad gets out first, "Robert, you wait here. Norma may be chasing a bear," says Dad as he grabs a stick that is lying near the shore.

I hold the boat steady while Alice and Mom get out. Norma's bark becomes a somber howl, which echoes sadly from the forest. The summer breeze halts, the birds take flight —time loses all meaning.

"Does a bear have her pinned or cornered against the rocks? Is she dying? Where are the pups?" I call out to Dad.

Dad doesn't answer me. After an agonizing length of time, Dad slowly comes out of the woods. His head is bowed down. With all his might, he throws the stick he is carrying into the lake. He does not look at me, only looks at Mom. "Robert, best you don't go after Norma. She needs time. The pups are dead."

In a heartbeat, I blindly run past my Dad into the woods, driven by inner disbelief. The sound of Norma's pathetic whimpering guides me to her. I drop to my knees at her side. My tears stop flowing onto my cheeks, bypassing my eyes; they begin to flood around my heart.

The strings which hold my heart, break one by one, and then my heart slips into my stomach. My arm comfortingly goes around Norma, pulling her closer to me. She is cold. I feel her tears fall onto my hand, and we cry together.

My father approaches from behind me, touching my shoulder. I can't recall what is said as he walks to the tree. I watch him reach up to a branch and unwrap the snare wire from each of the pup's necks. He set the puppies on the ground in front of Norma.

"Dad, why would anyone want to hang two innocent little puppies?"

* * *

That evening, with Norma at my side, I dig two small graves near the cabin. Mom gives me two of her finest silk kerchiefs that she wore to church to wrap around each of the pups. Norma crouches on her stomach while I cover the graves with my hands. I know she understands what I'm doing when she sadly sighs and puts her face between her paws. I watch as the sparkle disappears from her eyes. Alice is on her knees, consoling Norma. As he does on so many Sunday evenings, Dad reads from the Bible as I hold my mother's hand.

Taking the blanket and pillow off my bed, I sleep next to Norma by the pups' graves. When I wake, sometime during the night, to turn over, I look toward the cabin and see Mom and Dad sitting at the window watching me. It seems as though the moon this August night wipes its tearful eyes on the passing clouds and skips its next lunar phase, sending its full glow onto the pup's graves. Oh, how my heart goes out to Norma as she mournfully whimpers through the long night.

Chapter 20

Dawn comes quickly. My blanket is heavy with morning dew, and I'm feeling chilled. I wipe my eyes with my fingers, knowing this was not a dream but bitter reality. I pet Norma, offering words of comfort, then proceed to the cabin. Mom and Dad act as though they just got up, but I know different. The smell of coffee warms my thoughts as I go to my room to put my pillow and blanket back on the bed.

The carriage is soon loaded, and we are on our way to the train station. There are few words spoken this morning; we are a family in mourning —held together by a bond of love.

Dad doesn't look toward Redson's Store as we pass through Singers Glenn. I can't help myself and take a peek toward the store. Scagg Redson is standing outside the store, watching us go by. He doesn't wave, just stands there watching the carriage pass. Somehow, I have the feeling that his blank look suggests he already knows what happened.

The lonely train whistle echoes through the Hollows of the Appalachian Mountains as it chugs around the bends, working its way into Harrisonburg. With my nose pressed against the train window, I stare out, looking for answers. I know only God has the answer to why. I start to write a message in the fog my breath has left on the window. A note I started that day and have added to as events, as well as tragedies, unfold in my life, entitled 'Dear Heart.'

I can't wait for the crate to open so I can hug Norma. My parents and Alice took a carriage from the train station. I choose to run home with Norma.

* * *

Like clockwork, the leaves fall to the ground as autumn approaches, smothering the sidewalks with their colours. Without straying, the geese stay true to their southern routes. The red squirrel in the oak tree listens to nature's call and gathers acorns for the winter.

School bells ring in the morning air. It is nice to be back with my friends. We have a new teacher this year, Miss Hamel. It is her first class, and she looks relatively young. Her red hair flows below her shoulders, and at times she pins it back. Her freckles seem to inspire one to smile when she looks at you. Her dresses fit snuggly, and she proudly stands tall in her high heels. When she bent down to pick a piece of chalk off the floor, she captured all the boys' attention as a bit of her ample bosom showed. Yes, she sure has all the right stuff.

Rebecca and I became closer that summer. I start holding her hand more often when I walk her home from school. Sometimes, I have to switch hands when her books become too heavy.

Fall slipped into winter, and the winter comes in like a lion, silting layers of snow onto the city. Cold winds drift off the mountains, the school was closed for a few days in January, but that is to be expected every winter.

Spring comes late to Virginia this year, as does the greenery of the city. The trees hold back their leaves until after the last spring frosts. The grass in the yards remains lifeless, waiting patiently for rain. Norma becomes incredibly nervous and distant as the weather warms. When I go to school, I tie her to the apple tree in the backyard to keep her from wandering off. At night she stays in my bedroom with me. The plan is working, and I think Norma is getting over her nervous agitation.

Sadly, I recall the day as if it were today when Alice went outside without closing the front door behind her, and Norma ran out onto the street. I called and called her, but she never looked back —she kept running.

"She has to go, son. It's nature at work," Dad says, putting his hand on my shoulder.

I kick at the sidewalk, mumbling swear words to myself. Sitting on the front porch with a lantern, I stay up all night wrapped in a blanket, waiting for Norma to return. Rebecca stays with me for a time. The city streets get quiet, and one by one, the lights go out in the bedrooms of the homes in the neighbourhood. Soon we hear Rebecca's mother calling her to come home. She stands and squeezes my hand tightly, wiping her tears away with her other hand. And, on that lonely night when I felt that I'd lost everything dear to me —Rebecca kissed my cheek.

* * *

The bell rings for the final time, and school is out for the summer. My arms are full, carrying Rebecca's books, so I didn't get to hold her hand this day.

Mom and Dad were planning a trip to the cottage, and of course, they invited the Hardie's. A few weeks later, both families board the train to Singers Glenn. Rebecca sits next to me on the train as it winds its way through the mountain passes and forests of pine. I look out the window, letting my thoughts drift, only feeling sadness. My mind is filling with questions that need answers. The closer we get to Singers Glenn, the more I want to go home.

Previously, Dad had made arrangements for someone to pick us up at the train station. Mom, Thomas and Ada Hardie, along with Alice and Rebecca, went ahead in the first carriage. Dad and I stop at Redson's store for supplies.

"Good to see you, Arthur," Scagg says to my father as they shake hands. Dad reads off the list Mom had given him, while Redson sets the items in boxes, and I carry the boxes to the carriage.

"Tell me Scagg, what's the latest news," asks Dad.

Redson looks at him. "You must be referring to the Haggards. Umm, Orie Dodge told me that Teress Haggard died during the winter. That poor woman, she's finally found peace. There was no service or funeral. Orie said that Edsel and Delilah dug a grave in a spot she always loved to visit."

Dad nods, "What about Edsel and Delilah? Who watches over them?"

"No one. Everyone is afraid of those two. Edsel and Delilah bear Eva Smir's curse. They both run wild, stealing what they want. There are rumours of missing dogs, cats and other farm animals. The Jeffers kids were beaten up and cut with a knife by them a week ago."

"Does Singer Glenn have any policing or law here?" Dad asks.

"Once a month, two officers come on the train from Harrisonburg. They go back the next day. It's just routine for them, and no one dares to open their mouths. We have to live here."

"Robert, take the last of the supplies your mother wanted and wait for me in the carriage," says Dad with a determined look on his face.

Putting the box of supplies in the carriage, I wait for my father. The horses are restless as they swipe the flies away with their tails. Through the window, I can see Dad in conversation with Redson. He points to a gun in the display case. It's a Colt pistol. Dad pays Scagg for the supplies and stuffs the Colt into his jacket pocket, along with a box of bullets.

Arriving at the cabin, I help unload the supplies and luggage from the carriage. I wave to Rebecca to come outside and join me. We walk to the graves of the two pups.

"Dad, Dad, come here," I say, waving excitedly. Dad and Thomas Hardie quickly run to me. "Look! Look at the tracks; Norma was here."

"You're probably right, son. I suspected that's why she ran off."

"That means she will come back to me," I say with a smile.

"Robert, don't get up your hopes of Norma coming back. From what I heard and read about animal instincts when something traumatic happens to them, they go rogue. They become independent and lose the bond of relationships. They become the hunters, not the prey," says Thomas Hardie as he reaches for Rebecca's hand. We all remain silent, staring at the graves, wondering.

That evening I move my bed against the window, watching to see if Norma will return. I fall asleep and awaken as the sun rises above the pines. Quickly I run outside in my pyjamas to see if there are any dog tracks around the burial spot. Sadly, there isn't.

During breakfast, Dad and Thomas talk about going fishing on the lake after they have their coffee.

"Robert, would you like to come fishing with us?"

"Dad, really. After the last fish that I caught, do you think I should try again?" Thomas and my father chuckle. They do not want to hurt my feelings and don't comment on the boot I caught last summer.

"Wish us luck, Katherine," says Dad, closing the door behind himself.
I walk with them to the boathouse, carrying a small basket of food my mother and Ada prepared for them. We slide the boat to the edge of the water, and I take my fishing rod from the bottom of the boat. The hook is still attached to the small boot.

"I'm going to show Rebecca how to cast with the fishing rod," I say as I walk into the boathouse. I find a pair of pliers to unhook the boot from my line. Fumbling with the pliers while steadying the boot, the hair on the back of my neck stands. My breathing momentarily stops. My eyes widen as I stare inside the boot. The hook is snagged onto a faded white sock that remains attached inside the leather boot.

I quickly step out of the boathouse to get my father. I am too late; he and Thomas are fishing in the middle of the lake. My thoughts run wild. Whose boot is this? Why is there a sock in the boot? Did my fishing line pull it off someone's leg? Is there a body at the bottom of the lake?

Covering the small boot with a rag, I push it behind a box on the top shelf. My interest in showing Rebecca how to cast is gone. I put the rod and reel in the corner of the boathouse, then sit on a pine stump, watching my father and Thomas as they fish. The words that Redson said run over and over in my mind. Now I wonder if the Curse of Eva Smir has its hold on our family.

Chapter 21

The invitation extended to the Hardie family to join us at the cabin every summer at the end of the school year became a tradition. The summer of 1901 was no different. I turned 16 at the beginning of June, and Rebecca wasn't too far behind me. We would be celebrating her birthday at the lake on the 14th of July. She had blossomed into a beautiful young lady, and with every moment we spent together, we grew closer.

Our kisses are more intense, and when I hold her in my arms, I can feel her melt into me as if we have become one. Her soft brown hair always tickles my nose when I whisper in her ear, and we do a lot of whispering and giggling. Intercourse is just a word. That word somewhat scares us. What Rebecca and I have is more significant than any single word. We share a feeling of true love —that very few find.

Alice is still a pest. She has grown up quickly and is now talking about boys from school. One evening, I overheard her asking our mother to invite Henry Peel and his family to the lake. Of course, Mom said she will have to discuss the matter with Dad. I know Henry from school and don't care for him. I wonder what Alice sees in him. He always seems to be picking his nose. His nickname is Nose Peel, but I don't recall anyone calling him that to his face. Henry's mother, Dolores, sings in the church choir. His father, Bristol, works for the Harrisonburg Gazette. Now, Alice's dolls remain at home on a shelf, and her secretive diary is always nearby, and she often goes to her bedroom to write in it.

Dad has entrusted me to harness the team of horses to the carriage. I can see him watching from the cottage window as I tie the team to the horse railing. He comes out of the cabin with Thomas and hands me a list, saying, "Get these supplies from Redson's. Thomas will be going with you; he has a few letters to mail."

"Rebecca, are you coming with us?" I ask, with a grin on my face and my chest puffed out, excited that I'm driving the team.

"Not this time, Robert. I'm helping in the kitchen."

Rebecca waves to me as she stands on the steps. I shake the reins, saying, "Giddy-up, let's go." It isn't long before we drive up alongside an older man strolling on the road, carrying a stick. The man is tall and lean. He seems a bit nervous when we stop. He has an old wide-brimmed hat on his head, with a band of dried sweat soaked through to the outside. He isn't wearing a shirt, just a pair of loose-fitting overalls with patches on the knees, giving him the appearance of a scarecrow. It looks as though he hasn't shaved for some time. His beady steel grey eyes only glance at Thomas and me for a second. Then he looks away.

Thomas says, "Hello. Would you like a ride into Singers Glenn?"

The man ponders, rolling a stone along the bottom of his boot and then kicking it off the road. He throws the stick in his hand toward a stand of pines and climbs into the carriage. There is an offensive odour coming from him as he sits down. Thomas nods to me, and I gently slap the leather reins on the horses' backs. No one speaks, and for a time, the sound of horses' hooves and carriage wheels on the small stones are comforting and rhythmic. I occasionally look over my shoulder at the stranger. He notices me looking at him and quickly shifts his eyes from me. I feel at ease with him.

Thomas turns, "I am Thomas Hardie. This lad next to me is Robert Billings." Thomas reaches out his hand. The man does not shake it.

"Umm, Orie. Orie Dodge," the stranger says, wiping his lips with his hand. "Billings. That name, I've heard it before. You're the ones that bought the timber rights around the county and have the house by the lakeside."

"Yes, that's right," I say, looking at Orie Dodge. "My father is the vice president of Virginia Lumber and Milling. Thomas also works for the company."

Orie becomes quiet. I sense he feels a bit out of place. "Mr. Dodge, do you live near here?"

"Just back down the road where you stopped for me, a half-mile or so in the Holler, alongside Dickson Creek."

"Dickson Creek," says Thomas. "That area has good stands of pine. But, if I recall correctly, the surveyors said that if we began cutting there, the spring runoff would cause the creeks to overflow and flood the Shenandoah Valley."

"Oh, yeah, I heard that too," says Orie.

I stop the horses at the Parcel and Post Office, letting Thomas off. Thomas tells me to go ahead, and he will meet me at Redson's store. Orie and I get out of the carriage at the store. He waits while I tie the horses.

"Robert," he says, a bit embarrassed, looking to the ground. "Would it be too much to ask if I can get a ride back with you? Those feed bags get heavier every year."

"Yes, of course, Mr. Dodge," I say to him.

"Call me, Orie. I'm no Mister," he says. For a moment, there is a hint of a smile on his face and his steel grey eyes warm. Feeling his friendship as he puts out his hand, I shake it. Then follow him into the store.

"Dodge, what brings you into town?" asks Scagg Redson, happy to see his friend.

"I had a craving for the black licorice sticks. Or did you eat them all again?" chuckles Orie.

Redson smiles, taking the lid off a large jar and handing Orie a paper bag. "Robert, grab a few of these. Don't worry. They're compliments of old Scagg," snickers Dodge.

I feel comfortable being in the company of these two men. They are lifelong friends, taunting each other like kids on the playground at recess time. I hand Redson the list my father had given me as I chew on some licorice. He fills two boxes with supplies and sets a box of bullets for father's Colt handgun on the counter. "Do you want the bullets in your pocket or the box?" asks Scagg.

"You can put them in the box," I answer and begin carrying the boxes to the carriage.

"Since young Robert has offered me a ride home, I'll take three bags of feed, the ones with molasses added to them," says Orie.

"Orie. Do you have a goat that is ready for butchering?" asks Scagg. "I could take half of one at any time. Just let me know, and I can come one Sunday after church to help. Oh, by the way. Who has eggs for sale around the area? Mrs. Hutcherson took the last dozen this morning."

"Thought you were getting eggs from Edsel and Delilah," says Dodge, grabbing another licorice from the jar.

"I don't need any more trouble from those two. They're stealing the eggs they bring to me. Higgs told me he saw them running out of his chicken coop the other evening with some eggs and said there was a dead chicken with its neck wrung. He took a few shots at them but missed. Them two are getting damn scary," says Redson.

"Since Teress passed, they have turned wild. They cut the throat of one of my goats a month ago —just to watch it die. Good thing I was home and heard the commotion, so I was able to salvage the meat. I gave them a scolding, but they ran off laughing. I should off taken a switch to them."

My heart is still aching from what the two Haggards did to Norma's pups. I want to add to their conversation but know it would be out of place. It's not the time to bring up old memories since I'm an outsider.

I carry the last bag of feed for Orie, throwing it on the back of the carriage. Thomas is in conversation with two men across the street. He notices us preparing to leave and shakes hands with the two men. He sets the package he is carrying on the seat of the carriage and climbs in.

The sun is favourable to us on the trip home. The gentle breeze rolls off the mountain top and through the whispering pines. The contented birds chirp back and forth, announcing us to one another. The horses' hoofs seem to be keeping time to one's heartbeat, and the smell of their leather harnesses seeps into my nostrils. It is a grand day!

I can see our cottage from the road as we get closer and stop the carriage allowing Thomas to get off. "I'm going to take Orie home and should be back within the hour."

Casually, Orie and I chat while we make our way to his farmyard. There is a pen made of peeled rails in which his goats run freely. A small building between the house and goat pen is his blacksmith shop. An anvil sits near the doorway on a large oak stump. Several hammers and a large pair of pliers lay on the ground near the stump. I set his feed bags beside the blacksmith shop.

"Hold up a minute," he says and walks into the shop, coming out with a jug of homebrew. "Robert, have a swig. I bet you're parched," says Orie grinning.

"No, thank you, Orie. My mother would tan my hide if she smelled brew on me." I climbed into the carriage and wave to him.

"Alright. You come by anytime, you hear," says Orie.

Chapter 22

The July weather was excellent for the remaining week, and on the evening of the 14th, we lit a huge fire by the lake. Mom and Ada had prepared a potato salad, and we roasted hot dogs. Rebecca was thrilled when her father came out of the cabin carrying a chocolate cake layered with icing. All 16 candles brightly flickered on the cake. Tickled and excited, Rebecca made a wish and blew out the candles. I hope she got her wish. Later that evening, we gathered around her and sang, 'Happy Birthday.' Rebecca began to cry.

In the morning, the Hardie's packed their belongings. I gave Rebecca a kiss behind the cabin and walked her to the carriage. Dad gave them a ride into Singers Glenn to catch the train. I stood on the driveway, waving to Rebecca. She waved back. I could still see her, yet I was already missing her.

* * *

"Mom, I'm going to take a piece of Rebecca's birthday cake to Orie. I should be back in a few hours."

"Robert, are you sure? You only met the man once. I don't think it's a good idea. Did you tell your father about your plan?"

"I'll be alright. Don't worry."

I walk down the drive, turning onto the main trail. The morning dew has evaporated, leaving a faint creamy coloured stain on the shrub leaves. The clumps of berries hanging from the branches have lost their tint of green and are swelling into delicious, looking purple berries. I'm not sure if they are safe to eat, so I decide not to taste them.

Noticing Orie working by his forge, I walk directly to him. Handing him a bag, I say, "Orie, I brought you a piece of my girlfriend's birthday cake."

"Well, Thank you. I won't turn down a nice piece of cake."

We exchange some small talk back and forth for a spell. I sit on a block of pine while Orie goes to the well and pulls up a bucket of water. He takes the dipper hanging on one of the poles, which supports the small roof and has a drink, throwing the excess to the ground.

We continue talking, "Well, umm, I guess I better get home. Dad may need me." Then, having gotten up my nerve, I apprehensively blurt out, "Orie. My father and I were fishing a few years ago on the lake, and I snagged a child's boot. What seems really strange is there was still a sock inside the boot."

I quickly glance at Orie. He turns red and becomes agitated. There is a moment of silence, then he brings his hand up to his jaw, rubbing his face. "What were you hoping to catch? There are no fish in that lake, only sand crabs and eels," nervously says Orie.

"Yeah, we never did catch any fish. But the kid's boot that I snagged has always been on my mind. Was there ever anyone missing from the area?"

I know I struck a nerve as Orie sidesteps the question. "I reckon there are more than just boots in that lake. I used to skinny dip there in my younger days. Gretta Moore saw me swimming in the lake once and hid my overalls when she was passing by. The water got cold, and I had no choice but come out of the lake. I was naked as a Jaybird. Gretta warmed me up quick," chuckles Orie, reliving the moment in his mind.

I can see his eyes brighten, and his ageing body finds a bit of swagger once more when he recalls the romance he had with Gretta Moore. Somehow, I feel that Orie knows the story of the kid's boot in the lake. Perhaps I am making too much of nothing.

Mom and Dad talked me into joining them at the cabin once more before school starts. Rebecca and her mother are on a shopping spree in Richmond, and I am happy they'd taken Alice with them. She has gotten over Nose Peel, claiming Billy Wilder is the new love of her life. She chatters about Billy constantly; at least he doesn't pick his nose all day.

I go to see Orie once more before we leave for the city. I knock on his door. This is the first time I've entered his house. He is sitting at the table, sipping shine and smoking a cigarette. He points to a chair, and I sit down. "My father would appreciate it if when you walk into town, you do a walk around at our cottage while we are away. Every time we come back, tools and other stuff have gone missing. Once, the doors to the boathouse were open, and Dad's fishing rod had disappeared."

"I would bet a silver dollar that you know who has been snooping around there," says Orie as he pushes the can of tobacco nearer and pours a glass of shine for me. I stare at the lid on the can of tobacco and visualize my mother's face as she shakes her index finger at me.

"Yeah, probably those Haggard kids," I reply and begin telling Orie what happened to Norma and her pups. I have to wipe the tears from my eyes a few times while telling the story, but knowing I'm talking to a friend, I'm not embarrassed. Orie puffs on his cigarette, sipping on shine while he listens. Without thinking or realizing what I am doing, I take a drink from the glass. My mouth is on fire as the moonshine trickles down my throat, burning the sorrow locked within me. I sneeze several times, and my chest hurts when I take a breath. Little stars are dancing around in front of my eyes as I try to focus. I feel good —and take another sip.

To this day, I can't recall what else Orie and I talked about. But I do remember the scolding I got from my mother and father. That night, I slept with a pail next to my bed.

* * *

The school bell rings once again as we crowd the hallways looking for our assigned rooms. All the boys are happy to see Miss Hamel sitting at the desk when they walk into the classroom, including me. She looks more comfortable and confident this year.

That afternoon when she drops a piece of chalk and bends forward in front of my desk to pick it up, her bosom is delightfully exposed to me. Her perfume infuses itself into my mind as my eyes widen. I am mesmerized.

Unexpectedly, something strange happens to me. My underpants become soiled with an unknown liquid. I feel squirts ejecting from my stiff penis and cross my legs quickly, trying to hide the protrusion in my pants. Then a flush of red infiltrates my body, and I become weak. Sitting at my desk, unable to move, I don't know what will happen next.

I pray that Miss Hamel will not ask me a question, or God forbid, tell me to stand. It seems to be an eternity before the 4 o'clock bell finally rings; moving quickly, I am the first one out of the school doors this day. I go straight home to change my clothes and wash off the gooey stuff sticking to my skin like cement and smells like fish.

* * *

The fall season catches the red squirrel off guard. It scurries through the first snow looking for its winter supply of acorns. The leaves fall with the snow, mixing like an inedible salad, then freezing solid. Winter has descended on Harrisonburg with a vengeance. Christmas is the typical back and forth with visitors and supper invitations.

My stocking is full, along with a few surprises, especially the half dozen underpants from Mom. I wonder if my mother somehow knows of the predicament I was in at school that day?

Alice is still chasing Billy and working on her second diary. Our Dad had the biggest surprise, telling us that he is now the President of the Virginia Lumber and Milling Company at Christmas Eve dinner. Mom is shocked by my Dad's news and abruptly excuses herself from the table, going into the kitchen. My father follows her —a heated argument ensues.

Chapter 23

The warm breezes drift from the Atlantic Ocean and over the peaks of the Appalachian Mountains. Streams and rivers collect the spring runoff, delivering nature's gift to the fertile land of the Shenandoah Valley. The apple tree in the backyard shows promise with fresh new shoots. Encased blossoms buds, held hostage during the winter, release their colourful display, calling the humming bees. The oak and sycamore trees that adorn the sidewalks are true to time, adding their share of beauty to the city. Sadly, the chattering red squirrel that called the oak tree home isn't anywhere to be seen.

My father's new position at the Lumber and Milling Company keeps him at the office many evenings. He has new goals and wants to expand the mill. Mom, Alice and I usually eat dinner without him. There are times he leaves for work very early in the morning before Alice and I are awake. Mom has become more involved with the church, organizing events. She continues to sing with the choir, even though her voice has lost some of its lilting quality. Alice finally fasces reality, admitting to herself that Billy Wilder has no interest in her. Mom and I joked about it a few times, wondering who Alice's next supposed boyfriend will be.

Rebecca's mother, Ada, took ill that spring, becoming bedridden and needing constant care. Rebecca missed many days of school in the last month. Thomas began taking lengthy times off from work, tending to Ada. A rift between my father and him grew. Dad eventually demoted him. Rebecca and I remain close, but there is tension building between us.

Boarding the train for Singers Glenn on a cold rainy day in July, I am travelling alone. Mom has a church event that she needs to attend. Dad has become trapped in the world of business as the State of Virginia finds new prosperity.

Sitting on the same seat that I sat in many times before, I feel alone and empty inside. I wonder what Rebecca is doing and if I am on her mind. She definitely is on mine.

The new prosperity of the surrounding counties is visible from the train window. Telegraph poles line the train tracks to Channel Rock and through to Singers Glenn. The silver wires hanging from pole to pole carry the good news of the day, along with the tragedies. The state is evolving, but the backwoods, which so many call home remain devoid of progress.

Stepping off the train onto the walkway at the train station, I walk toward the Telegraph office. I stop to watch the train as its whistle sends clouds of steam into the damp air. Writing a note on the telegraph office stationery paper, I hand it to a man sitting at the desk. He asks for 25 cents. I can hear the dots and dashes leave his clicker and imagine the dots competing with the dashes for space in the small wire. Amazing! I think to myself.

Old man Higgins is standing at the doorway of the livery stables. I hand him the $40.00 Dad gave me to pay for boarding the horses during the winter. Queenie and Belgium are restless after the long winter and want to run. I hold the reins tightly, coaxing them to maintain a slow trot to Redson's store.

"Hello, Robert," says Scagg as I walk into the store. "Where are your folks."

"I came alone this time. Dad has a project at work, and Mom is involved with the Church social. I need supplies to tide me over for a few days. What's new in Singers Glenn?" I ask.

"Living in the city, I guess you don't hear any of the news from here. Old Molly Ryerson was murdered just before Christmas. You may not have met her. She lived closer to Channel Rock than Singers Glenn."

"Murdered?"

"Yeah, it was really gruesome! Someone chopped off Molly's head and arms in her own house. Then, the house was set ablaze."

"Really. Wow! Did they catch the person?"

"No, they didn't. That's not all. Some folks told me they found calves and dogs with their throats cut. Someone seems to love killing, for the sake of killing," says Redson, shaking his head.

On our way to the cabin, the horses are anxious to run, and I allow them their freedom for half a mile then hold them to a trot. I find contentment in the smell of their leather harness in the midday sun and talk to Queenie and Belgium like they are old friends.

Unlocking the front door to the cabin, I put the groceries on the kitchen counter. The window next to the back door is broken. Someone was in the cabin. I go directly to my mother and father's bedroom. Opening their closet door, I find my father's hidden Colt pistol and the box of bullets.

I disembark from the buckboard, tie the horses by the water trough, then knock on Orie's door. From where I'm standing, I can hear him shuffle and slide his chair back. When he opens the door, I take a step back. The intoxicating smell of moonshine awakens my memory.

"I was wondering when you would show," says Orie with a grin.

"Here's a can of tobacco. Redson said it's your favourite, and I got you a bag of the black licorice sticks you like."

We sit at the table making small talk. Orie is in a drunken state and often repeats himself. He keeps insisting I have a drink with him. I politely refuse, remembering how sick I felt after the last time we had drinks.

"You know. I've been thinking of what you told me about the boot you caught in the lake. I do recollect something that may be related. It was years ago when the young Moffitt girl got lost in the woods. Their folk's homestead is down in the Holler, seven or eight miles from here. Everyone believed she was attacked and dragged off by wolves. I had my suspicions at the time."

"What suspicions?" I curiously ask. Orie rolls a cigarette and ponders for a moment. I patiently wait for his answer as I slide my chair closer to the table.

"Well," says Orie, scratching his head as he lights a cigarette. "It was about the time when Beau and Edna were running wild. That was a lot of years ago, if I recall correctly. They were as thick as thieves, them two, and roamed the woods like wolves. It was something Beau said to me one night when I was courting his mother, Teress. He was hard to understand at the best of times. Anyways, he kept saying, 'katty, katty, that was

126

good.' He repeated it several times while his hand squeezed his cock through his trousers. Edna just covered her face, laughing and agreeing with him. It was years later that I found out the Moffitt girl's name was Kitty."

"You mean, Beau may have killed that girl and thrown her in the lake?"

"I would be willing to bet on it. Edna was always at Beau's side. At times, I could have sworn she was the Devil's daughter. They loved to kill birds, animals, anything, just to watch it die. Then they would chop their kill into pieces, laughing as they chopped."

"Whatever happened to Beau and Edna?"

"That's another story. One I feel is best left alone," says Orie, obviously disturbed and saddened.

I realize that he is drunk and slurring his words, but I honestly believe him. We go outside, and he says, "There's something about moonshine that makes me piss like a horse." Chuckling, I have a piss also.

"Yep," says Orie as he shakes his cock before slipping it back into his trousers. "I sure miss Teress. Them older women do make better lovers." For a moment, his thoughts get lost, and he stares toward the sky, smiling to himself.

"I best get back to the cabin. Someone broke in during the winter, and I have a mess to clean up," I say to Orie as I do up my zipper.

"I saw the broken window when I went to check on the place for your father. You do know who it was, don't you," says Orie, giving me a serious look.

"Yeah. I'm pretty sure it was Edsel and Delilah. Edsel left a trail with his jackknife, cutting up our family photographs. Rebecca, my girlfriend's picture, was taken from the frame which was on my nightstand."

"Them two are a pair cut from the Devil, far worse than the seed they came from. I should have done things differently then. I knew from the moment I first saw them —they were born under Eva Smir's curse."

Stunned by his comment, I ask, "What did you mean by that? You make it sound as if Beau and Edna are the parents of Edsel and Delilah."

Orie looks at me with his cold, steel grey eyes, "They were."

Speechless, I try to comprehend his comment. I never heard of such a thing, not even in the animal world. Somehow, I feel I'm being watched from above and in need of absolution to clear my unsavoury thoughts.

Chapter 24

That night, I sleep with the Colt under my pillow. In the morning, I clean up the glass from the floor and find a few boards in the shed to cover the broken window.

From the kitchen window, I can see the boathouse doors are open. A wooden storage box that holds a few tools is lying on its side a few feet from the open doors. Bending down to flip the box over, I suddenly jump back—my hand fumbles for the gun in my pocket. Aiming the gun at the storage box, I stand there shaking slightly. A raccoon runs out from under the box and into the shrubs. I breathe a sigh of relief; thankful I didn't shoot myself.

That evening, I sit on the large stone near the lake, watching the water's silent ripples tickle the shore. The comforting sunset slowly drops and disappears below the Shenandoah Valley. All the while, I'm wondering what Rebecca is doing. The moon's silhouette appears as the sky darkens and covers the lake like a comforting blanket. The stars are hiding tonight. Perhaps, they have been given the night off.

The next morning, I put my father's revolver back in its hiding spot. Feeling lonely, I pack my bag and head for the train station. Once aboard the train, I put my head against the window in hopes the motion along the twisting rail tracks will let my mind run away on an adventure.

It is late afternoon when the train arrives in Harrisonburg. I catch the trolley car to Jefferson Street and Fourth Avenue.

Mom hugs me when I walk into the house, "Was there a good turnout for the church social?" I ask.

"Yes, it was fun and profitable. We managed to raise a tidy sum."

"That's great, Mom. I'm going to go see Rebecca."

I knock on the Hardie's door, then knock again. Thomas opens the door but does not greet me with a smile. He gruffly calls Rebecca. She comes down the stairs, and we walk outside together. I reach for her hand, but she abruptly pulls it away, saying, "My mother is very sick. I really need to get back to her." Sadly, Rebecca walks toward the house. It's obvious her mother's illness is taking a toll on her. My efforts to comfort her are rejected. Not knowing what else to do or say, I keep my distance.

I didn't hear from or see Rebecca until her mother's funeral three weeks later. I offer my condolences but feel they went unheard. Mom and Dad try their best to comfort Thomas and Rebecca in their time of grief.

* * *

My parents never did make an effort to go to the cottage that summer. Their lives had somehow changed. My dad became very influential in the community. He had the opportunity to run for State Legislature, representing Harrisonburg and surrounding counties. In the fall, he won the nomination by a slim majority.

With his briefcase in his hand, Dad catches the train to Richmond on Sunday evenings. A telegram often comes on Fridays, informing Mom that he is staying through to the following week.

Mom moved Dad's clothes into the spare bedroom. There is a tense emptiness in our home. Even when Dad is home, both Alice and I feel we are walking on eggshells.

My mother's work at the church is taking more of her time. She remains a vital part of the church choir and social functions. Father Benson asked her to relieve him of the Sunday School lessons. Talk is, the good Father enjoyed blessing everything with church wine. By the time classes got started, he would be slightly inebriated or having a 'Holy Rest,' as he called it.

Alice grew out of her boy crazy phase. She set new goals in life, planning to enroll in University after she graduates. Alice and Dad are like two peas in a pod, always talking about the law and legislation bills. Once, when she was writing in her diary, I glanced down as I walked by, seeing 'Alice Billings Attorney at Law,' written on a page. My little sister is becoming a young lady.

I only get to see Rebecca once again before school starts. She is waiting for her father to arrive, then they plan to go for groceries at Murphy's General Store. She looks rather tired. The colour has disappeared from her face as well as her glow, which at one time tickled my desires when she looked at me.

Finding my courage, I ask Rebecca, "Would you like to go out together some afternoon?"

"Um, Robert. I don't think I am ready for dating. Father needs me more, now that my mother is gone."

I squeeze her hand. It feels cold, and she doesn't respond. I walk home, feeling I've lost Rebecca. Perhaps she has lost herself and doesn't have the inner strength to rebound back to life.

* * *

The golden yellow and crispy red leaves clutter the streets once more. Autumn winds that sweep in from the Appalachians have a cool briskness as they force their way into the city. The oak tree, which was once home to the red squirrel, and where I carved Rebecca's and my initials, remains bare throughout the summer. The old relic has lost its will, and a city worker painted a white X on its trunk.

The school bell rings through the city again, recalling the students as a new school year begins. Miss Hamel got married during summer break. Rumour has it; she is pregnant. She no longer wears snug fitting dresses nor bends down to pick up the chalk that occasionally slips from her hand. She merely slides the chalk against the wall with her shoe.

Rebecca's desk remains empty for the first two weeks into the school year. When she eventually returns to class, she keeps to herself. She seldom waits for me after class, which would allow me to carry her books home. When we talk, it is about the day's lesson or homework.

Thomas and Dad have mended their past dispute. Mom invites Rebecca and her father to Christmas dinner. After dinner, we sing Christmas carols and open our gifts. A lone gift remains under the tree, wrapped in white paper and tied with a red bow. Alice walks to the Christmas tree. Smiling, she hands the gift to Rebecca, who is hesitant to open the present.

Rebecca unties the ribbon while looking at her father and opens the box. Smiling, she removes a red dress with white lace around the neckline from the package. She is delighted with the gift and runs to her father, kissing his cheek.

"You best read the card, Rebecca. The present is from the Billings' family," says Thomas, pleased to see his daughter smiling again.

"Rebecca, come to my bedroom and try the dress on," says Alice.

The bedroom door opens in a few minutes, and Alice steps out, announcing, "I give you, Miss Rebecca Hardie."

There is a hush in the living room. My mom puts her hands together, then presses her fingers against her lips as her eyes sparkle at what she sees. Dad and Thomas stare at Rebecca and smile. I stand, silently staring at her. Her eyes have once again found the glow which had vanished. Rebecca's smile lights up the room, reigniting an ember within me. Her hair comes alive as it sways on her shoulders when she walks to the centre of the room. The red dress fits perfectly, awakening desires that were lying dormant in my mind.

I walk to her. I can feel a vibrancy emanating from her. "Close your eyes, Rebecca," I say, stepping behind her. My fingers are sticky and nervous as I take her present out of my shirt pocket. "Are you sure your eyes are closed?"

"Yes, Robert, they are," giggles Rebecca.

My sweaty hands cross over and pass one end of a gold chain to the other hand. Rebecca's breath tickles my hands as I slip the necklace around her neck. My nervous fingers fumble against her skin, trying to clasp the two ends of the chain together. I can feel a flush of bumps rising on her neck. A craving, an urge, begins to grow in my pants. I want to kiss her neck but step back as she turns and hugs me.

Rebecca runs to the mirror in the hall. She takes the heart-shaped locket that is attached to the gold chain and rubs it between her fingers. Her smile widens while staring into the hall mirror. She turns to me with a look that I will never forget, then kisses my cheek. I sense the Rebecca I once knew is back.

The slight distension within my pants settles but returns later that night with a hardened determination. That night, my pillow has a heartbeat of its own as I smother it in my arms, pretending I'm holding Rebecca while drifting off to sleep.

* * *

Our love for each other grows with each passing day. We are inseparable through the remainder of the school year. I carry her books home from school every day, and Rebecca's hand is always in mine as we cross the street together. A deep sexual craving is stirring our appetites for each other, pulsing through our bloodstream, like a runaway train. Right or wrong, each touch, each kiss, grows into a hunger for more.

We ignore what our parents tell us and what we learned in Sunday School. We tempt fate, exploring the forbidden. Inevitably, our intense feelings and passion overwhelm us — we become one.

Chapter 25

The school bell rings for the final time for Rebecca and me. We both graduated with honours. The summer of 1903 begins, filled with excitement and promise. I apply to the University of Richmond to further my education, and I am accepted. I plan to take business courses and criminal science. Rebecca enrolls in a nursing course at Richmond University. We are excited; the future, like the sun, grows brighter each day.

I catch the train to Singers Glenn in the first week of July. As I did so many times, I sit in my favourite seat, looking out the window. It's become a habit I can't resist; to push my nose against the window, fogging it up with my breath. I draw a heart on the steamy window, printing Rebecca's name inside with my finger. A chuckle can be heard from the seat behind me. I'm embarrassed that someone was watching and turn to see who snickered at me. A well-groomed, attractive lady smiles at me. I'm captivated by her beauty and elegance.

She says, smiling, "I am glad to see romance is still alive. Your Rebecca is a lucky young lady."

My dry gaping mouth closes, but my eyes continue to stare. The lady enthrals me. She may be older than me, but her beauty causes erotic thoughts to flood my mind. My eyes undress her within a few precious seconds. Her scent awakens all my senses, filling my mind with desire. Her tongue slowly glides over her red lipstick as she waits for a response from me. I break into a nervous sweat, awkwardly saying, "Um, Rebecca and I recently graduated together. We have been dating for a long time." I quickly grab my jacket to cover the hard-on that springs upward in my trousers.

She stands and politely asks, "May I join you?"

"Yeah. Sure, of course."

I cross my legs, keeping the jacket draped over my lap. The lady extends her hand to me, "I am Claudette." I shake her hand and introduce myself.

When she removes her white linen gloves and puts them in her purse, I notice she isn't wearing a wedding ring. I avoid eye contact. It feels like a rush of hot blood is pounding through my veins. "Where are you going?" I ask.

"I live in Richmond, but I was born in Harrisonburg. I'm here for my father's funeral. Both my mother and father are now gone."

"I'm sorry for your loss." There is a moment of silence. Claudette pulls a linen handkerchief from her sleeve and wipes her eyes. The train's whistle blows as we pass through Channel Rock. I look out the window, feeling a bit uncomfortable and ashamed for letting my thoughts run away with me.

"Tell me, Robert, where are you going?"

"I'm on my way to Singers Glenn; our family has a cottage by the lake. It's a beautiful spot overlooking the Shenandoah Valley. I'm going to check on the place. Hopefully, there is no winter damage. My parents may not be coming to the lake this summer."

My thoughts begin to wander, and I am dream wishing while blindly staring out the window. For a moment, I fade into my

Sir Lancelot story, and something inside of me hopes that she will invite herself to the cottage. Silly me, why am I even thinking like this? There is something about the train that lets my imagination get the better of me.

The train whistle sounds as we round the bend, "This is my stop," I say to her. I stand and excuse myself while squeezing by her, getting to the aisle. Reaching above her for my travel bag, I look at her. Claudette's enticing smile is holding me hostage, and I want the train to keep going.

"Robert. If you're ever in Richmond, please look me up. We can go for dinner," she says, handing me a business card from her purse. I stand on the platform of the train station and wave to Claudette. She waves back. The train pulls away, sounding its whistle as short bursts of steam dissipate in the air. Setting my travel bag down, I look at the card in my hand: **Claudette Chandler, The Richmond Sun, 1066 Riverdale Street**. Slipping the business card in my wallet, I make my way to the livery stables.

Queenie and Belgium are anxious to get going as old man Higgins hitches the team to the carriage. I drive the team to Redson's store. "Good to see you, Robert," says Scagg. "Are your folks not with you?" he asks while setting a cardboard box on the counter.

"Not this time. I came alone to check on the cottage. I'm not sure how long I'll be here." Walking through the store, I gather supplies and place them in the cardboard box. Grabbing a paper bag, I fill it with black licorice. Scagg smiles at me and sets a tin of tobacco in the box. "Orie will appreciate the licorice and tobacco. He's slowed down a bit. I haven't seen much of him this summer."

"Scagg, tell me, what about the two Haggard kids. Are they still running wild?"

"Worse than that. It's believed that last month, the Haggard twins pulled the Hobson girl into the bush when she was walking to Singers Glenn. She was badly beaten and cut with a knife. The cuts to her body are too gruesome to describe, and the unthinkable happened; she had been raped. She hasn't spoken since the ordeal, and they think she may have gone mad. That poor girl! We all know who beat and molested her, but without her testimony, no arrests can be made," says Scagg. "The county finally stationed an officer here. Um, Kelsey is his name. His office is a few doors down from the Telegraph. Not much he can do by himself."

"That's awful! So, if the Hobson girl doesn't speak, nothing will be done about the Haggards. Oh, my God! I hope she's not pregnant with Edsel's seed," I say to Scagg.

On the open road, the horses break out into a trot. Their hooves keep time in unison, like a well-tuned clock. The tall pines sway in the day's breeze as if whispering to each other. I slow Queenie and Belgium's pace, allowing them to cool off as we make the turn into the lane.

From nowhere, a squawking raven flies over the carriage spooking the horses—the bird lands on a leafless branch of the sycamore tree next to the stables. The fidgety raven flaps its wings and squawks at me while I water the horses from the lake. I feel uncomfortable with the bird and throw a stone at it to scare it away. The bird continues to watch as I put the horses in the stable. Once in the cottage, I hear the raven land on the roof.

There is no sign of entry or damage to the cabin during the winter months. Going into my parent's bedroom, I take the

Colt from its hiding spot and put it in my pocket. I make two cheese and bologna sandwiches, then walk to the edge of the lake to eat. The sun has begun to retreat into the western horizon, sending an orange reflection onto the calm water. The day's breeze halts and a silent eeriness sends the chill of the evening upon me.

* * *

The winds off the mountain guide the clouds downward, and a drizzle begins to fall, wetting the road. I stop the team and pull the top over the carriage. Puddles form on the trail and begin to pool together, then run to the side of the road. I tie the horses to the rail by the well and walk to Orie's door. He opens the door before I knock, "Good to see you, Robert," Orie says, leaning on a cane.

"What's wrong with your leg?"

"I thought those damned Haggard scoundrels were about and after one of my goats again. When I went to check, I tripped over a branch in the woods and fell on a rock. The gun went off. Them two devils ran like jackrabbits," says Orie, as he hobbles back to the table and pours a drink of shine for himself.

"I heard about what happened to the Hobson girl from Redson. What a bloody shame," I say, setting the tin of tobacco and the bag of black licorice on the table.

"Everyone has their guns loaded in case the Haggards show. Somehow, they don't understand right from wrong and must be put down. No one will ever know or care," says Orie, slipping his fingers into the bag and pulling out a licorice stick, then chewing on it.

"I haven't forgotten what you said last time we talked, that they are a pair cut from the Devil, far worse than the seed they came from. You said you should have done things differently then. That you knew, from the moment you first saw them, they were no good and under Eva Smir's curse."

"Yeah, I said that alright and meant every word."

"Do you think there is such a thing? That someone can put a curse on another person?" I ask, bewildered.

"You're damn right! I have seen it at work," says Orie, crossing himself in fear of reprisal from the curse or the Devil Himself.

"How did the curse begin? Who is Eva Smir?" I ask, pouring a few ounces of moonshine into a clean glass. Bravely, I take a sip.

"Teress was widowed when her husband was killed in the war. She was poor, with nothing and had no choice but to do favours for the menfolk. Jedediah Smir fathered Beau, that I know for sure. That was in 1867 or sometime thereabouts. Anyway, talk spread through the county like wildfire that Jedediah had fathered Beau. Eva, Jedediah's wife, waited for Teress to come into Singers Glenn. She got her revenge in Redson's store by throwing acid in Teress and Beau's face. That's when she placed her curse on Teress. It is a well-known fact that Eva practiced Witchcraft and talked to the Devil himself. Eva lives on —through her curse. The talk was that Jedediah threw Eva off the top of Whistler's Gorge, thus setting the curse into motion." Orie wipes his lips, rolls a cigarette and puffs. His hand slightly shakes as he relives the story he is telling.

"What happened next?" I ask curiously.

"A few years later, Teress gave birth to Edna. I'm not certain who Edna's Father was, but I believe she was Jedediah's child also. Teress kept Beau and Edna hidden from everyone. The people of Singers Glenn knew of them, but the children were kept out of sight, and they never got into trouble. She kept them in line, but she never realized they were committing sins between themselves."

Orie stops talking for a moment, wipes his forehead and takes a sip from the cup. Staring at the floor, he continues, "Teress killed Beau when she caught the two of them having intercourse. Edna died, giving birth to Edsel and Delilah. I saw them soon after they were born, disfigured, you know, from being inbred. Then those two babies were struck by the instant heatwave just after their birth. It may have affected their brains and their way of thinking. I know, the heat from the sun knocked the bejeebers out of me."

"What kind of instant heat wave?"

"Well, it was something I have never seen the likes of before. I would have sworn the Good Lord Himself was taking His vengeance out on Teress and me for all of our sinful fornicating. The twins were in a basket sleeping outside the doorway. Teress and I were in the cabin, well, you know."

Orie takes another drink then says, "Within a heartbeat, my ears were ringing like crazy. The ground rumbled, shaking the cabin, and I began feeling dizzy. I heard thunder in my time, but nothing compared to this; the whole mountain roared in pain as though it was being blown up. The heat came instantly and was unbearable. I passed out, and so did Teress. Only the Good Lord knows how it affected those babies, but they came back to life after their bodies cooled. Teress wanted to kill them. I shouldn't have stopped her."

Orie becomes quiet. Sweat drips off his nose and falls to the table. He wipes a lone tear from his eye as he pushes his chair back, looking down at the floor. I remain quiet, with no words of comfort— Orie relives the nightmare.

Chapter 26

The week goes by quickly as I put myself to work, chopping down a few dried-out trees in the woods. Using the horses to drag the tree trunks closer to the cabin, I then saw them into firewood. The boathouse door requires mending, as the nails holding the hinges have worked loose. Finding longer nails, I fix the problem, hopefully keeping the pesky raccoon out. The raven slowly flies over me a few times while I'm mending the door. I'm annoyed and manage to empty the Colt pistol, shooting at the bird but miss with all six shots.

Another bologna sandwich for breakfast is on my menu. Looking at the calendar, I realize it's July 14th, and I smile to myself. After harnessing the team to the carriage, I go into Singers Glenn. My first stop is the Telegraph office. I put 50 cents down on the counter. The operator relays a message to my mother, telling her I'm alright and unsure when I will be returning home. Smiling, I compose a Happy Birthday message for Rebecca, telling her I'm thinking of her and miss her.

The man behind the desk takes my money, and with the clicker, sends the dots and dashes into Harrisonburg. I walk the horses to the Livery Stables and water them. Higgins treats each horse to a scoop of oats from a pail. Old Higgins and I sit and chat for a while, then I pat Queenie's neck and walk to

Redson's store. Scagg Redson is busy at the counter with a customer, so I browse through the store while waiting.

"What brings you into town?" asks Scagg as he passes by me carrying a box of groceries for a customer and setting it in their buckboard.

"I needed a few things. I'm a bit tired of bologna sandwiches," I say, chuckling as Scagg returns.

He smiles and puts a can of Klunk on the counter, "Try this, it's a new brand of canned meat. I got a few cases in, and it's selling really well. How is Orie doing?"

"He hurt his leg when he tripped, but he's okay, and we had a good visit the day I saw him. Give me another can of Klunk. I'll drop it off for him, along with a bag of licorice." I begin to fill an empty paper bag from the counter with the black licorice that Orie likes.

Suddenly the Telegraph Office employee rushes in. "Glad you're still in town, Mr. Billings," he says as he takes his glasses off and hands me a telegram.

Glad everything is alright at the cottage. Rebecca was so excited to be going to see you. Alice and I saw her off at the train station yesterday. Mom.

My mouth drops as I reread the telegram. "When was this telegram sent?"

"Just a few minutes ago. I saw your team at the Livery and knew you were still in town. Is there something wrong?" asks the Telegraph operator.

"Are you positive that this is the correct wording? Rebecca, she's my girlfriend. She never arrived here yesterday. When is the next train from Harrisonburg due?" I ask in a panic.

Scagg quickly comes to my side, takes the telegram and reads it. "Rex, send a message to Harrisonburg and get confirmation on this telegram. I am going to the train station with Robert."

Scagg locks his store, and the two of us quickly make our way to the train station. He opens the door to the ticket office, "Henry, did a young lady get off the train yesterday?"

"Yes. Yeah, one did."

"Well, did she say anything to you or tell you where she was going? Did she have a ride?" I ask?

"I remember, she was wearing a red dress and carrying a small luggage bag. She didn't say, nor did I ask where she was going or how she would get there. Is something wrong Scagg?"

Scagg takes the telegram from me and hands it to Henry. The expression on his face changes, "You're Billings, are you not?" asks the ticket agent.

"Yes, I am."

"Now I recall the girl. She was back and forth with her folks a few years ago. Um, right. She and her folks used to vacation at your parents' cottage. Yeah, that's the same girl who got off the train yesterday."

My mind whirls out of control, going blank, to the point where I can't think. My heart slows and skips a beat, then pounds in my chest. My stomach is queasy. I feel weak and put my hand on the desk to support myself. I look at Scagg; he looks at me. We are both thinking the same thing.

"Henry, go and get Officer Kelsey. Now, Henry! Robert and I will be at the Telegraph Office," says Scagg.

I run to the Telegraph Office. The look on Rex's face tells me what I don't want to hear. "I'm really sorry, Mr. Billings. The message is confirmed. She was on the train yesterday."

Scagg walks in, taking control, "Robert, I suggest you get to your cabin and check. She may be there. When Officer Kelsey gets here, he can begin going door to door in the village. Get going, Billings. You're wasting daylight. I'll be along shortly."

At the Livery Stable, Higgins helps me hitch the team to the carriage. I slap the leather reins across the backs of Queenie and Belgium, and the horses dart onto the road. They continue at full gallop for over a mile. Their lungs are near collapse, and I can feel the pounding of their hearts through the leather reins. The hot, frothy breath expelling from the horses' mouths sticks to my clothing as I stand in the carriage, coaxing them, begging them to go on. White foamy sweat from their black coats covers the harness like a blanket of turbulent snow. Their hoofbeats fall out of rhythm. Queenie is limping slightly as she runs, but Belgium continues to run fast, tightening the harness, keeping Queenie in stride.

I can't keep doing this to them. I must bring them to a stop slowly, or they will soon drop dead. I pull back on the reins; they slow to a canter, then a complete stop. Both are coughing, trying to catch another precious breath. I tie the reins to the carriage, leaving plenty of slack. Petting both their manes, I thank them for doing their best. A teardrop from Queenie's dark eye falls onto my hand as I pet her.

Taking the gun from my pocket, I grip it in my hand and run down the road. Looking back, I can see the horses are slowly following along the trail. My mind is racing faster than I can run. The sweat from my brow is burning my eyes, and my chest is heaving, gasping for air. The pines along the road are whispering secrets to each other that only they can interpret.

Images of the Haggard twins are hiding behind every rock and bush. Their dirty faces are staring, laughing, poking me with their fingers as they make fun of me. I have to stop and catch my breath, but something inside me drives me to go faster. Flashes of darkness momentarily block my vision every time I blink. Every step brings more pain. The ache in my side is burning as if it were on fire.

The roof of the cabin is visible through the sycamores. Forcing myself to push on, I fall to my knees. Finally catching my breath at the driveway, I have a clear view of the cottage. My eyes scan in all directions, hoping Rebecca is by the lake or sitting on our favourite rock. I can't see her. I call her name. Once more, I call, but there is no response.

I almost piss myself! From nowhere, that fuck'n raven lands in front of me. It is squawking, flailing its wings at me, almost like it's trying to chase me from the yard. I stand, kick dirt at the bird and run into the cottage.

"Rebecca, Rebecca, are you here?" My calls are in vain and go unanswered— as do my prayers.

The pain in my side is unbearable, and I lay on the floor helpless, rolling back and forth. Each agonizing second passes slowly as the pain envelopes me, one heartbeat at a time. Nauseated, I spit on the floor, feeling I may throw up at any second. And then, vomit erupts from deep within.

The one too many bologna sandwiches are staring back at me from the floor. I continue hacking, feeling my intestines sliding upwards in my throat. I can't breathe. Purples and blues dominate my sight. I roll onto my back, feeling the sticky wet vomit dribble down my cheek and pool on the floor.

Chapter 27

My breathing subsides. Feeling as though I'm locked in a time warp, I spit on the floor, then wipe my drooling mouth on my sleeve while getting up slowly. I almost throw up again, seeing the mess on the floor.

Cradling my stomach in my hands, I go through the kitchen and out the back door shouting, "Rebecca. Rebecca." A raccoon runs between my legs as I open the doors to the boathouse, scaring the Hell out of me. I call into the silent forest of pines for Rebecca, only hearing my rebounding echo. Stubbornly, I run back to the cottage, checking and double-checking each room. She is nowhere to be found.

As I frantically run down the road, the sound of horses' hooves can be heard in the distance. Two buckboards come around the bend. Scagg Redson is in the lead wagon. "Any sign of Rebecca?" he asks.

"No, I can't find her. I looked everywhere. There is no sign of Rebecca being at the cabin. Are my horses alright? I pushed them pretty hard."

"They're not far behind us," says Scagg, reassuringly.

Without thinking, I say, "We need Orie. He knows them Haggards better than anyone."

Scagg agrees and says, "Carter, go fetch Orie. We'll continue searching along the road."

* * *

Sunset comes early that July day. With it comes the realization that our search may be in vain. The sky shrouds over, covering the face of the moon, leaving us scared of our own shadow. An empty helpless feeling hangs over everyone. The cowering pines no longer whisper their secrets— perhaps it isn't a secret anymore.

Queenie and Belgium stay true, pulling the carriage that brings every available lantern and citizen from Singers Glenn to help in the search. It is well after midnight when I send Rex back to the Telegraph Office to relay a message to my Mom in Harrisonburg and message Dad in Richmond.

Wanting to help, the ladies of the village gather at the home of Mrs. Albright. They prepare a constant supply of hot coffee and sandwiches for the volunteers, searching for Rebecca.

At dawn, the solemn sound of the lonely church bell rings. Its far-reaching resonance stops everyone where they stand. Orie, as well as Redson, remove their caps. I sense they are beginning to lose hope of finding Rebecca. In the midst of this tragedy, I feel another heartstring break.

We proceed to walk the road for miles in both directions, looking for signs of a scuffle or broken branches, but nothing. No blood, no clothing. It seems as though Rebecca has vanished into thin air. Extensive searches of the Haggard's shanty and farm turn up nothing, not even a trace of Edsel or Delilah.

The morning sun fades into the distant sky, covered over by a procession of clouds. The tormented skies rumble, perhaps in anger, releasing tears in the form of rain. No rainbow colours appear once the skies clear. Only a greying mist accompanies the chilling breeze.

* * *

The train rounds a bend, and three long whistles sound as it comes to a stop. My father steps off the train with four Federal Marshalls and half a dozen police officers. They immediately board the waiting carriages and come directly to me on the country road. For the first time in years, I hug Dad and cry on his shoulder as I did so many times in my youth. Fighting back his tears, he takes off his overcoat and gives it to me. After he shakes hands with Redson, I introduced him to Orie.

A Marshal starts asking me questions faster than I can answer them. Somehow, I believe he knows the answers. The Marshalls and police officers split into two groups and walk the road looking for clues.

The sun begins to set on this eerie, terrifying part of the Appalachians when the search is called off for the night. Dad convinces me to get into the carriage with him. Three Marshalls and Orie join us. The rest of the search party climbs into Higgins feed wagons, following us to the cottage. Dad stops at our lane and shakes Orie's hand once more. Orie gets out of the carriage and walks toward his home, still searching.

As we pull up to the cabin, I quickly run ahead to clean the vomit off the floor before anyone comes in. We rummage for leftover food from what the ladies provided. The men sleep two to a bed, and a couple of the men spend the night on the floor.

I dig through my travel bag, finding my notebook and the letter I started to write many years ago. Sitting in a chair at the kitchen table with the flickering lantern light, I begin to write,

'Dear Heart.'

'Somehow, out in the misty night, I can hear you calling. My heart reaches into the shivering darkness to answer. I call and call your name. But, no one answers.

My lonesome thoughts continue to fall in love with you, deeper than the day before. And my lonely heart is alone once more. I am so lonesome and empty without you, and cannot give in to my tears, as I wonder where you are.'

Dad wakens me at the kitchen table, takes the pencil from my hand, and sets it down. The aroma of coffee brewing wakes my senses, and I rub my dry eyes while looking around. I wasn't dreaming; the nightmare exists.

My father sits at the table with a cup of coffee. His hands roll the coffee cup back and forth, "Robert, we are going to do everything we can to find Rebecca. Son, please, don't give up hope. Hope is all we have at the moment."

I stand and stretch, looking out the kitchen window. The Marshalls and police officers are having coffee outside and sharing the two cans of lunch meat. "It has to be the Haggard twins that grabbed Rebecca. You heard of what they did to the Hobson girl?" I say to Dad, feeling a lump in my throat.

"Yes, I heard. It's horrible, but just speculation at the moment. The Haggards haven't been caught with blood on their hands.

Let's get going. We have to find them," my father says as he gets up from the table and gives me a reassuring hug. The pat on the back Dad gives me lifts my spirits, reminding me of what family means.

The morning sun is rising above the horizon. Dad and I step onto the front steps. The men only look at me from the corner of their eyes, not knowing what words to say that could comfort me. Some of the men are checking their rifles and pistols. Officers begin harnessing the two teams of horses to the carriage and wagon. I walk directly to Queenie and Belgium, petting their manes and talking to them like they are my only friends.

When our carriage gets to the main road, Orie is sitting on a log waiting. Men get off the carriage and wagon at quarter-mile intervals and begin sweeping the forest floor. As we get further, one can hear the men shouting back and forth to each other. Wagons and buckboards are coming towards us from Singers Glenn. The Marshalls take control, assigning each group to a search location.

A Marshall and police officer get out of the carriage as we get closer to the Haggard place. They go through the bush holding their rifles close to them. We stop at the overgrown laneway. Another wagon stops alongside us, and two officers get out. Each goes on either side of the lane. The wagon continues down the road, and another officer gets out.

Within minutes they all descend on the Haggard farmyard. They go through every dilapidated building, root cellar and shanty. A Marshall waves us to come to the secured yard site. Orie is quiet and waits by the carriage. I can tell he is overwhelmed with memories and perhaps ashamed.

Dad and I walk into the shanty. It's a disgusting mess! The blankets on the bed look crusty, like discarded cardboard. The pillows may have been white at one time but now resemble rocks covered in dirt. A nail on the north wall holds what may have been the last dresses Teress and Edna wore. There is dried blood on one dress, most of which has flaked off and fallen to the floor. Empty jugs of moonshine are piled in the corner. Tobacco tins and burnt pots clutter the table. The date on the calendar is from 15 years ago. Catching a glimpse of myself in the broken mirror held by a rusty wire twisted around a nail in the wall —I don't recognize the man in the mirror.

Dad takes the lid off the stove. Slipping his hand down onto the coals, he says, "Men, the Haggards were here approximately 12 hours ago."

Chapter 28

The men quickly split into two groups. They slowly walk the surrounding bush line looking for trails, marking them by leaning old deadfall and branches against the closest tree.

I look toward Orie, who is leaning against the carriage wheel, holding his cane —his face has lost all expression.

"Orie, you know them, bastards. Where would they take her?"

"Um, it depends on what they want to do with her," he says, looking directly at me.

Another heartstring breaks. My dry mouth hangs open, and my mind whirls in disbelief. I turn away from Orie, so he won't see me wipe the tears from my eyes.

Orie turns to my father and says, "You best get old man Higgin's hounds out here and a few shovels."

"Shovels! Do you think those bastards would go so far as to murder her in cold blood and bury her out here?" asks Dad, horrified by what he heard.

Dad and a Marshall are soon on their way to Singers Glenn with the carriage. I stay at the Haggard yard site with Orie and a police officer. The remaining group splits forces, and they begin walking the different trails.

I follow Orie down the slope. I can hear the trickling of water making its way between the rocks. "This is Dickson Creek. It's fed from the mountains up yonder and flows into the Shenandoah Valley. This is where Edna gave birth to Edsel and Delilah. I suspect, beyond the pines to the west, is where Edna and Beau are buried. Most likely, Teress' body is there also," says Orie, tapping his cane against a rock. Quietly, and sadly he adds, "The past is a dangerous place to revisit, for an old heart."

* * *

The overhead clouds are rolling back further and further, allowing the sun to do its part and control the day. The midday breeze is almost nonexistent along the water's edge, sheltered by the pines and oak trees. There is a stale odour in the air from the green slime clinging to the rocks in the creek. Cattails flourish downstream and have taken over the western side of the stream.

Stepping carefully on the rocks, I cross the creek and climb the slight embankment on the opposite side. The air suddenly changes the further I walk into the thick stand of pines. Sunlight fails to reach the ground through the intertwined overhanging pine branches. "You best wait up, Robert. I can hear Higgins' dogs. They're almost here," hollers Orie.

Crossing the creek to join Orie, we walk toward the approaching wagons. Higgins crawls into the back of the wagon and unties three hounds. One by one, the dogs jump off the wagon with a twelve-foot rope trailing each of them. Higgins gathers the ropes in his hand and walks the hounds into the shanty, letting the dogs sniff the bedding. The hounds start to bark and howl inside the house. The dogs have Edsel and Delilah's scent.

Dad is coming down the lane with the carriage. I wait and grab Belgium's bridle as the team comes to a stop. A Marshall gets out of the carriage, "Men, we have sandwiches and coffee. Let's have a bite to eat before we get started."

Rebecca's father, who was seated next to Dad, gets out. "Mr. Hardie," I say. He walks past without acknowledging me.

Dad approaches me, "Let's grab a sandwich, Son. Pay no heed to Thomas. We have to be understanding of how he feels. He needs to come to grips with the situation."

"Where do you want to start?" shouts Higgins, over the sound of the barking dogs.

Quickly, I approach the Marshall, telling him where Orie said there might be graves. The Marshall agrees. Higgins and his dogs take the lead, and we cross the creek like a herd of stampeding cattle. The hounds are in their glory as they pick up the scent, dragging old Higgins between the pines. Two dogs run to the left side of an oak, while the younger hound goes to the right. "Billings, here take the rope, you run Hawk. He's young and full of piss and vinegar."

I run alongside Higgins, between the trees and shrubs, keeping the rope snug as Hawk leaps over the deadfall. Hawk wants to take over the lead, but I pull him back. The hounds stop at a rock formation, circling each other, seeking the scent once more. The Marshalls and police officers go ahead of us, checking the crevices and hiding spots between the large rocks. Two officers clumsily climb the rocks and scan the area.

The hounds are off again, taking us over a smaller boulder and around spindly shrubs. We come to an open meadow. In the distance, a doe spots us and retreats into the forest with her young. The birds flutter into the air, frightened by the barking dogs. Everyone slows to catch their breath, but the dogs are anxious to continue.

Higgins takes the lead through the tall grass. In places, the dandelions and bluebell flowers have overtaken the grass. The yellow and blue colours, for a brief moment, give one's soul contentment.

The dogs abruptly stop at the base of a sycamore tree. We stand silent, looking at two sunken holes that are side by side. There is a growth of sparse grass growing on the sunken graves. Two wooden crosses that bear faded and peeling white paint have fallen to the ground. Next to the sunken holes is a grave with a small mound of dirt protruding from the ground. No cross marks the grave, only clumps of dead and dried flower stalks rest on the mound. Orie steps forward. Removing his cap, he crosses himself. No one says a word. Even the hounds settle and sit, despite what they discovered.

After a few moments, two Marshalls approach Orie, standing on either side of him. They are talking quietly, as though they do not want to disturb the dead. Orie points to the sunken graves, then to the grave with the dead flowers. From what Orie has told me, I know which is Teress' grave.

One Marshall walks to Higgins, "The scent that the dogs are following, how fresh does it have to be?"

"In my experience with these dogs, I would say within a week."

"So, we can say that they have been this way within the last week?"

"Yeah, that's a safe bet. But I would say within a day or so, by the way, the dogs were acting. I am going to walk the dogs around the meadow and see what they find," says old man Higgins.

"It's not up to me to decide what to do with these graves. Best, we go back to the yard site and follow up on the other trails." says the Marshall.

"Orie, come here," shouts Higgins.

Everyone walks to Higgins and the barking hounds. "Orie, the dogs picked up a scent. It looks like it goes down the gully and over the top of the mountain. Where would that end up?"

Orie turns, looking around as he gets his bearings. "Um, that goes over the mountain and overlooks the Shenandoah Valley. I think there is a narrow old road up there, but one has to go through Channel Rock to get on it. It's sandy ground on that side. The Confederate Army cut Redwoods from there, way back during the Civil War. Bet it's only three miles from where we stand, as the crow flies."

"Let's get back, men," says a Marshall.

Taking hold of Hawk's rope, Higgins and I follow the men across the open meadow to the yard side. Orie and I remain with Dad near the carriage while the others explore more trails in the woods.

Thomas Hardie approaches me. His eyes have gone cold, and his face is expressionless as he says, "This is all your doing, Robert. Rebecca was the only person left in my life, and you took her from me."

"Now see here, Hardie. You have no right to talk to Robert that way. He played no part in her disappearance," gruffly says my father.

Thomas gets into the carriage and sits there, staring blindly into the woods. Orie looks at me and says nothing.

"We best get into Singers Glenn and check if there is any news or if any telegrams have arrived. I need to send a message to your mother," says Dad as we begin to make our way back to the Haggard farmyard.

Hesitantly, I walk to the foot of Teress' grave. My inner core trembles with fear. Nervously pondering for a moment, I say a prayer recalled from Sunday School in hopes of an answer. Silence prevails. I turn and follow Dad and the others back to the carriage.

The sun has dulled and lost its warmth as though in mourning. Tall grass in the meadow whispers like an unconducted choir. The yellow tears of the dandelions drip from out of the petals, down the quivering stems and pool at the base of the plant — blue belles bow in silent prayer.

Chapter 29

Queenie and Belgium trot along the hard-packed country road. The sound of their hooves echoes in my empty heart. Dad stops the horses whenever we come upon townsfolk searching on the trail or in the woods. The questions and answers are always the same that there are no signs of Rebecca.

Thomas insists he wants to return to the train station. Henry, the ticket agent at the railway station, comes out the moment he sees our carriage. Once again, the questions and answers are repeated.

"Okay, Thomas, we will talk soon," says Dad. Thomas gets out of the carriage. He doesn't say a word, just sits on a bench waiting for the train. His demeanour and the look in his eyes are that of a very distraught man.

Dad ties the team to the horse rail at Redson's store and walks to the Telegraph Office. Orie and I go into the store.

"Robert, Orie. Um, I just got back myself. I dropped off the empty food baskets at Mrs. Albright's. The women said they will have more sandwiches and coffee made soon," says Scagg Redson.

"Scagg, I can't thank you enough for your help," I say.

"How's your leg, Orie? Take this tin of salve and rub it on your leg tonight," Scagg says, handing him a small can.

"The Hell with waiting till tonight? I'm going to use it right now. My leg is killing me," says Orie as he sits down on a keg of nails.

Dad walks into the store with a telegram in his hand. "Your mother is worried sick over this. I had no choice but to let her know that we haven't found Rebecca yet," says Dad, looking at me. "We better take some food with us. We don't know who may be staying at the cottage tonight."

"Dad, I want to walk to the cottage and keep looking along the road. There has to be something we are missing. I should be home before dark. See you in the morning, Orie. Thanks again, Scagg," I say while leaving the store.

Dad follows me to the steps. "Son, if you confront the two Haggards, don't hesitate to use the revolver," he says as he watches me walk away.

* * *

I pick up a stick from the roadside. Walking with it in my hand comforts me, perhaps in the same way my blanket did when I was young and would drag it around the house with me.

The bright blue skies do not hold a single visible cloud as the sun delivers its constant light. In all directions, the horizon remains silent about what it has witnessed, unable to disclose what occurred. The choir of birds that once sang from the treetops along the road have disappeared deep into the forest. The pines remain standing tall and still, without swaying. Their shiny green needles extend to catch the sun's warmth. Clumped together, the branches of red willows reach upward, sending their long narrow leaves as offerings. One would think they're in prayer.

Three men in a buckboard, pulled by a team of chestnut horses, aim their rifles in my direction as they get closer to me. "Who are you?" asks the wagon driver.

"Billings. Robert Billings," I say quickly.

"Sorry, Billings. We are from the next county and heard what happened. I am Jock DeFerr, and these are my sons, Adrien and Gaston. We came to offer our help. We had our share of grief in our county from the two Haggards. It's time we put a stop to them and their evil ways."

"We have no definite proof it is them, but everything we know about Edsel and Delilah points to the two. The law agrees and is looking for them as well." I say to the men in the wagon. The driver tips his hat to me, slaps the reins, and they move on.

Still carrying my stick, I continue walking on the road. Occasionally I walk into the forest looking for broken branches, trails, or signs of a struggle but find nothing out of the ordinary. I manage to make my way back to the cabin before the horizon swallows the sun.

* * *

I reluctantly take my father to the train station that cold, dreary Sunday morning. We say our goodbyes, shake hands, and Dad hugs me. Our muddled thoughts can't find adequate words of comfort, but tears inside both of us trickle over our troubled hearts. I wave to him from the station platform, sadly watching the train round the bend. The search for Rebecca has come to an end.

Queenie and Belgium pull the carriage through the quiet village. From a half-mile away, I can hear the hollow ring of the church bell. Its somber tone cuts another precious heartstring within me.

I turn the team onto the narrow street and follow the sound of the calling bells. When I open the church door, the people that are gathered inside turn to look at me. There is a hush. The only sound heard is the squeak of the door as it closes behind me.

I'm feeling captive in a large jar, and someone just closed the lid. Fighting the claustrophobic feeling, I sit on an empty pew. The preacher nods to me and continues with his sermon. I do not hear a word he speaks; I only sit in denial —waiting for a miracle.

* * *

In the days that pass, I receive a telegram from my father,

Son:
The news from home is not good. Thomas Hardie
was found dead in his home last night. He hung
himself. Your mother, Alice, and I miss you and
beg you to return home.   Dad

I hitch the team to the wagon and go to see Orie one last time before leaving. The weeks have taken a toll on him, as well as me. His hip is worse than before, and the ointment no longer helps. He seems more agitated than ever. I feel he's come to enjoy the company of moonshine more than mine.

He is not surprised when I tell him that Thomas Hardie hung himself, only saying, "That fuck'n curse! Mark my words, Robert. The curse of Eva Smir lives on."

We shake hands, and I close the door behind myself. I ponder for a moment, wanting to go back in to say something to Orie; but don't know what to say. An emptiness overcomes me as I walk away, knowing I may never see him again.

I never really paid much heed to Eva Smir's curse before, but as the horses trot to Singers Glenn, I put all the pieces together. Perhaps there is some validity to her curse.

Old man Higgins greets me at the livery stables. I ask him to take good care of the horses and proceed towards Redson's store. Hearing a whinny from Queenie and Belgium, I stop. Their call tugs at my emotions, and I return to pat them again.

Scagg Redson is behind the counter as usual. We chat as if we were lifelong friends. He promises to send me a telegram if he hears any news. Opening my wallet, I keep twenty dollars for train fare and give Scagg the remainder. "Keep Orie in licorice and tobacco." Redson smiles as we shake hands.

Heading back to Harrisonburg, I sit on the opposite side of the train, hoping to reverse my bad luck. The whistle sounds rounding the bend as it always has, and soon the train slows on an upward grade as though in slow motion.

My thoughts drift back to when I felt invincible, dreaming that I was Robin Hood, and Miss Clement was Maid Marion riding her horse alongside mine. How naïve I was. So much has happened since then. Oh, how I long for yesterday.

An overwhelming urge moves me to think; the Hell with superstitions. I push my nose against the window, allowing my breath to fog over the glass. Drawing a heart with my finger, I print Rebecca's name in the centre. She is alive to me and within this broken heart of mine.

I take the letter I'm writing to myself and write;

'Dear Heart:'

'There are so many dreams that will not be dreamt. So much aching love within, and now, never to be given. The taste of life is sweet, like your last kiss on my lips, and the call of yesterday blows blindly in the wind. OH, God, I beg Thee to answer my prayers.'

Chapter 30

The passage of time eventually settled my nerves and emotions, although the hurt never fully subsided. Our family became united and connected once more, but it took a tragedy to do so.

My father no longer slept in the spare bedroom. Mom often accompanied Dad to Richmond for the week, and at times they stayed the weekend.

Alice bloomed into a young lady. Her diaries remain in her top drawer, covered over with sweaters. She excelled in school and became head of her drama class. Not surprisingly, she graduated with honours.

In time, Dad resigned as president of the Virginia Lumber and Milling Company. He remains focused on the role he plays in the Legislature, getting bills passed that aid the citizens of the outlying counties. He eventually sold the house in Harrisonburg. I moved from my one-room apartment to the family's new home on the banks of the James River in Richmond.

* * *

Every summer, I go back to the lake cottage by myself. Neither Mom, Dad, nor Alice have the desire to return. Yet, something keeps calling me back.

For some years now, there are no visible paw prints around Norma's pups' graves. The grass has overtaken the whereabouts of the graves. I remain the lone visitor.

A destructive, new family of raccoons took up residence in the boathouse. The door I once fixed lies on the ground as rot weaves its way into the wood.

The child's boot that I caught that summer day, thinking it was a fish, remains hidden in the spot where I left it. On a bright sunny day, I take the shovel and give it a proper burial in a wooden box that Redson gave me. The box has 'Gummy Sticks' written on it in bold black letters. The spot I choose is at the edge of the lake, facing the day's sunrise.

* * *

Scagg Redson died of an apparent heart attract while stocking shelves in the store. Rumour has it that his Last Will stated he did not want to be buried next to his wife. When the train stops, I walk from the station and visit the Singers Glenn cemetery. Scagg's wishes are respected.

Orie is now an old man, and time has been unkind to him. His memory has faded, and he never mentions Teress or the Haggards anymore. I know I'm losing my friend. Orie's life and mind are now trapped in an old body.

* * *

I major in business and criminal science. Now free from the burden of four years of University, that summer I assist in Dad's campaign for re-election. He wins his seat in the Legislature with a clear mandate. I know he is grooming me to take over someday.

That day comes sooner than expected. Two years after his re-election, he suffered a stroke. He lost his speech and use of the left side of his body. He can communicate with us on a small chalkboard and clumsily prints on it. His health quickly deteriorated when pneumonia set in. Alice and I are in his room with Mom the evening he passed. Mom hands me the chalkboard with his last wish. It states, *"Burn cottage."*

Mom keeps herself busy in the house. Her work at the church is her source of solace, a place where she is among friends. She insists that Alice and I be home by 6 p.m. every evening to have dinner with her, and we better have a good excuse if we are late.

Alice's dream comes true. She passes the Bar Exam and is offered a position at the District Attorney's Office. She is delighted with the offer, but I believe she is more excited about seeing her name on her office door. At the dinner table, she often complains to Mom and me about the minor role she has in the office. Mom soothes Alice's ego, telling her all good things come with time.

My father's seat in the Legislature remains vacant. I put a lot of thought into running in the by-election and finally throw my name into the hat as the Republican candidate. I am green to politics but soon catch on. It's not what you know or can do; it's more a game of what you can promise. Crossing one's fingers behind your back is accepted in politics.

The campaign begins at the Richmond train station. I feel like a Ringmaster at the circus, standing on a small platform, waving my arms for attention. I'm telling the few people who stop to listen to me what I will do for them if elected. No one pays heed to me, and the passing trains continually drown out my voice.

The great campaign, as I refer to it, takes us through the counties and small towns. The passenger car has large white banners bearing my name printed in blue letters, tied on each side of the railcar. Red, white and blue ribbons hang from the banner. We whistle-stop in remote settlements, and I give my speech. Co-workers throw out handfuls of candy to the children. Other workers nail posters on telegraph poles, reminding the citizens to vote for me.

Deep inside, I'm embarrassed and feel like a salesman trying to sell something I know nothing about.

Chapter 31

Surprisingly, I win the election by a slim majority. Perhaps I won because my name is at the top of the ballot. My colleagues continually tell me, one must always be campaigning, especially when first elected. If you do not, don't count on getting re-elected. Madeline was my father's secretary, and she remains on the job as mine. She knows the ins and outs better than anyone, especially concerning the dealings of the Legislature.

I spend most of my first few weeks in the office looking for things to do. My new fountain pens and pencils are used mainly for playing Xs & Os with myself. Occasionally, Jimmy, the mail boy in the building, plays cards with me. Often, he wins more than his fair share. He keeps me in the loop regarding who is doing what or who is doing who.

Madeline's need for coffee is comparable to mine, and for a time, I become the coffee and doughnut fetcher. Eventually, I get appointed to a few committees. This is a way of earning my stripes and climbing the slippery slopes of politics.

Returning from another boring committee meeting, I set a cup of coffee on Madeline's desk. She smiles and says, "A columnist from the Richmond Sun wants to interview you. Straighten your tie and button up your jacket."

I walk into my office, closing the door. A lady sits in the chair facing my desk. The subtle aroma of her perfume causes me to stop, and for a moment, I'm held hostage to the fragrance.

Light from the window creates an aura surrounding her. Her blonde hair cascades from under the stylish blue hat and rests on her shoulders.

Hot coffee spills over the rim of the cup and trickles onto my fingers. I nervously walk to the side of my desk, set the cup down and glance at the street through the window, then turn toward the lady in the chair. A memory from years ago runs through my mind.

"It's you —the lady on the train. It's you," I excitedly say.

Puzzled, she looks at me and asks, "The train?"

The erection she'd given me then instantly springs back. As I cross my legs to hide the bulge in my pants, my foot hits the desk, spilling more coffee. I feel myself blush as sweat sweeps over me.

"Um, yeah. The train. We met on the train years ago. You came and sat next to me. Uh, you were on your way back to Richmond after attending your father's funeral."

"Oh, that's right, I remember now," she says, smiling, raising her hands in disbelief. "Oh. Wow! That was a few years back. You wrote a girl's name into a heart shape on the train window. Tell me, did the two of you get married?"

The rush of sweat that sweeps over me turns cold. I uncross my legs, and I'm at a loss for words. "No, we didn't," I say, sadly looking at the floor.

"I am sorry," she says, realizing her question upset me.

"Yeah, well. Um, that was then. We all have a past," I say. Opening my wallet, I pull out a worn business card and set it on the desk.

"How special! You kept my card all these years." Claudette's smile turns into a grin, then a giggle as we look at each other.

"I always knew that someday, our paths would cross again," I say, crossing my legs once more.

* * *

Our beaming smiles warm the night. The watching moon turns a shade of blue, covering its sight and shedding its jealous tears in a passing cloud. My heart continually skips a beat. I am a lost star, glowing as I slide down the Milky Way, perhaps like a falling star —but falling in love.

The taste of her skin on my tongue teases my tempted heart, like a candle flame flickering in the evening breeze, flirting with destiny. The night belongs to us; our fingers roam freely, each with a touch of its own. Our skin shivers while newly found delights and thoughts awaken, flowing like spring streams to a begging sea.

Each kiss, each touch ignites a new ember within our aching bodies. The intensity of our lovemaking continually peaks, taking us higher and higher each time. Our love flows freely and orgasmically. Love silts in, covering our locked hearts, and only we have the key.

The orange rays of the rising sun enviously dance on the window sill. A westerly breeze guides the last of the greying darkness away. Our naked bodies bathe in the warmth, but we wish for darkening shades of nightfall to return.

Then cheerful morning light shines brightly through the linen curtains in Claudette's upstairs bedroom, exchanging the fading orange colour and slowly blending into a contented yellow.

I kiss Claudette's inviting lips. My eyes become jealous of my melting lips. Again, her nipples harden against my chest. My fingers caress her silky hair as I kiss her eyelids. I inhale her arousing aroma, which strengthens my lusting thoughts.

* * *

As soon as the day's work ends, we become inseparable. The upstairs bedroom in Claudette's house is where we spend most of our time. Mom no longer gets on my case for not showing up for dinner.

I feel comfortable with Claudette. She possesses a rare compassion and has a unique way with words. I faithfully read her column in the Richmond Sun. When I stop at her workplace, I often look through The Sun's archives, reading her published stories.

"Claudette, I've been looking through past copies of The Sun's archived papers. I see Channel Rock and Singers Glenn were often in the news. Reports of missing children, mutilation of livestock. Who is Avery Whittington?"

"Whittington was a freelance reporter. The Sun would publish his articles when we had space."

"How can I contact him?" I ask.

"Um, come to think of it, I haven't seen any of his work for years. I can find out from our editor where he is."

That evening, after walking Claudette home, I tell her of Rebecca's tragic disappearance. She asks no questions, only listens sympathetically, then holds me in her arms.

A wound inside of me reopens. I feel an ache in my heart, reliving the events of that summer. My yesterdays, I never forgot as they remain vivid in my memories. Rebecca's warm hand that touched my heart, I still feel. Her last kiss, I still taste on my lips —and miss the most.

* * *

Like clockwork, fall slid into winter. The cold winds come off the Appalachian Mountains as expected. Freezing rain cements the city into a standstill for days at a time. It's a Christmas without snow, but Santa does bring me what I want and need. I propose to Claudette Christmas morning. We are to be married in the spring, and Mom insists the ceremony is to take place in her home.

On the 20th of May, a warm spring day, Claudette and I are married under the apple tree. The blossom petals replace confetti, falling delicately and sporadically. Alice blushes when she catches the bouquet. Her date from the office, Cecil Carrington, keeps his distance. Mom is proud and in her glory as most of her church group is in attendance. Madeline is outspoken as usual and gives a short speech. I am not sure if she wins any votes for me or costs me votes.

We spend the entire week of our honeymoon in Richmond's plush Jefferson Hotel. The massive bed in the Presidential suite becomes our playground.

I move in with Claudette. Her house is close to the downtown area of Richmond and within walking distance of her workplace. As time goes on, I gain respect from my colleagues at the Legislature. My portfolio, as well as my workload grows. Claudette finds approval among the staff and elected officials I work with and gets the inside scoop on any developing stories within the Legislature.

Chapter 32

Once again, it is time to hit the campaign trail. New banners are made and attached to the side of a railcar. Claudette is my biggest asset and joins me on the train. She writes my speeches, but I know the men are looking at her, not listening to me speak. Again, candies are thrown to the children and posters are nailed to telegraph poles and storefronts in the towns where we stop.

It's a damp rainy day as the train blows its whistle when we stop in Singers Glenn. There is no one standing on the train station platform. Looking out the window of the train, I can see a few buckboards at Redson's old store. Since the people are not coming to me, I will go to the people. Grabbing an umbrella, I walk to the store alone to sell myself.

Redson's sign remains, hanging above the door. I introduce myself to the owners and shake hands with everyone in the store. I ask what their concerns are, living in Singers Glenn. Instead of speaking, I listen to what they say. Mrs. Albright recognizes me. She steps toward me, and gives me a hug, then wipes her eyes, saying, "That poor girl, we never did find her."

The room goes silent. Mrs. Albright looks up at me with her sad eyes as the past runs through her mind. My breath fails me, like a blown-out candle in the wind. Words flee from my vocabulary. I clear my throat, "No, Ma'am. We didn't."

"This is a big concern in the county. Those two still roam freely. Everyone is scared to death of them," says Mrs. Albright.

"You mean Edsel and Delilah?" I ask.

Mrs. Albright replies, "Yes. They're back. Most believe that the Haggards never left, just moved around from place to place like animals. Months go by without anyone seeing them. The law caught up with them, but they have no proof of any wrongdoing."

"I promise to get more police officers stationed around the community, as well as Channel Rock." The train whistle blows twice. I quickly shake hands with everyone, set a silver dollar on the counter, and fill a paper bag with green gummy sticks.

* * *

I win the election and can keep part of my promise to Mrs. Albright. I manage to get a bill passed through the Legislature within six months. Funds are allocated for one police officer to be stationed in Channel Rock.

Two years into my second term, Cecil Carrington asked Alice to marry him. Mom insisted they be married at the house. Since the wedding, Cecil and Alice have lived upstairs in the house, and Mom resides on the main floor. Soon, they had their first child, a daughter. Her name is Peggy. A year later, Alice gave birth to a boy they call Arthur, in honour of our father. Alice remains at the District Attorney's Office, becoming the lead lawyer for the State.

Claudette and I are unable to have children of our own, but we can't get enough of Peggy and Arthur, especially at Christmas and birthdays. Wanting to be a family, we decided to adopt a three year old girl, Sara, and Claudette becomes a stay at home mom.

Alexis Crigg, the Senator who represents Virginia in Congress, passes away while holding the office. His seat is up for election. Encouraged by co-workers, I take on the challenge. Taking a leave of absence from the Legislature, I run for State Senator of Virginia.

Claudette, along with Sara, join me on the campaign trail. Banners are made, speeches are written and given, and the candy is thrown to the children. But after the votes are counted, Conrad Oth wins the election.

* * *

In June of the following year, Alice throws an elaborate birthday party for Mom. Our mother's entire church group attends, as well as most of Alice and Cecil's co-workers. Cecil and I put on aprons, barbecuing steaks and hamburgers. Mom's most treasured gifts that day are her grandchildren.

Alice takes me aside and says, "Robert, when you get a chance, I want you to come to my office. But call first. I may be in court."

"Sure, uh, tell you what, how's first thing Monday?"

"Good, we'll see you then."

Monday morning, I drive downtown and park my car across the street from the District Attorney's Office. I knock on Alice's open door and walk in.

"Robert, come in. Um, I hate to even bring this up with you. I know the Hell you went through when Rebecca disappeared," says Alice, as she leans back in her chair.

My legs suddenly go weak, and I sit down, asking, "Did they find her body?"

"No, Robert. But another child has gone missing in the Channel Rock, Singers Glenn area. A brother and sister who live together have been arrested. They are in jail, here in Richmond."

I take a deep breath and stand, "Is it them, the Haggards?"

"No, it isn't them. I have been working on this case since May. I interviewed these two several times. They did not do it, and I will instruct the court to release them this week."

"What makes you think it's not the two you have in jail?"

"No motive. No body. The two in jail may be illiterate, but I know these two are not murderers," says Alice, as she takes a sip of coffee. "Robert, sometimes I hate this damn job."

"I know what you're thinking, Alice. Those fuck'n Haggards remain on the loose. Everyone knows they're born killers," I sit, then stand and walk down the hallway. "Anyone have a cigarette?"

"Right here," says a clerk. I light a cigarette and walk back to Alice's office.

"When did you start smoking?" asks Alice.

"Just now!"

"I thought you should know; horrible things continue to happen in Singers Glenn."

"Yes, I know. I was reminded a few years ago when Mrs. Albright told me that everyone in the county lives in fear.

Alice, do you remember that day when we were with Dad in the Haggard's farmyard? Edsel's stare scared the Hell out of me, and Delilah ran off with your doll."

"Aggie," says Alice. "My doll's name was Aggie. Yes, I remember. I never forgot that moment."

Alice takes a tissue from her desk to wipe her eyes. I hug her, and she walks me to the doorway. "Robert, when was the last time you were at the cottage?"

"Um, I can't even remember. Time has a way of distorting bad memories."

"Did you follow through with Dad's last wishes?"

"No, not yet. I will, when and if I find the courage."

That night, sitting in front of the fireplace, I read the letter to myself, entitled 'Dear Heart.' I read of my fears and the nightmares that at times still torment me. The undying love I feel for Rebecca leaves me hoping she found her rightful share of Heaven. But most of all are the written words of the vengeance I still crave.

And now my hand quivers once more as I write, 'As God is my witness, I will get revenge for you, Rebecca.'

Chapter 33

In the following days, Singers Glenn dominates my thoughts. I tell Claudette that I am going to the cottage to check on its condition.

"Why now, Robert?" curiously asks Claudette. "Would it be all right if Sara and I come along?" she suggests.

"I don't think that would be advisable at this time. It's been years since I have been there, not even sure what to expect myself," I say, throwing a few items of clothing on the bed.

Claudette knows something is bothering me, so she ends the conversation by walking out of the room. I continue packing. Opening the closet door, I reach above the door casing and grab the box of bullets along with my Colt pistol, slipping them into my travel bag.

Once in Channel Rock, I stop at the inn for lunch. Not much has changed, including the unsavoury food. Getting back in my car, I drive along the narrow road and ignore the sign that reads Singers Glenn, going straight to the cabin at the lake.

I'm somewhat overwhelmed when I stop before the driveway and look at the glistening water on the lake. Memories of the life I knew then dance on the waters. A calm feeling overcomes me —moments from my youth and the dreams of yesterday rush through my mind. Then as I turn the bend, the

183

purples and blues continue to shine, calling me back to the dreaded time when Rebecca went missing.

The boards I nailed over the broken window years ago now lay on the ground. Tracks on the hardwood floor tell me traffic in and out of the cabin has been frequent; possibly it's been used as a hideout or stopover. There is a musty odour in the air that assaults my nostrils. I leave the front door open to allow a flow of fresh air. There are 14 notches carved into the kitchen counter with a jackknife. Their meaning is unclear, but I'm pretty sure it's the work of Edsel.

I drive my car around to the back of the cabin and carry my belongings inside. Lighting a cigarette, I sit at the kitchen table and put six bullets in the gun.

Nightfall comes quickly to the Appalachian Mountains. The air finds its crispness. I lock the front and back door, telling myself that I am safe here, but my skin wants to crawl away. I sit in the dark, blowing smoke rings into the night. The moon relinquishes its glow this night and is covered over with blankets of clouds. The stars are recalled from the Heavens, leaving the region in total darkness. Eerie winds whistle in the night and loosen a shingle —rattling my nerves.

The morning sun shines through the kitchen window, onto the table. Its light and warmth wakes me. I wipe my groggy eyes and light a cigarette, then look through my overnight bag, searching for a Coca-Cola. Its bubbly vigour awakens my senses.

While driving into Singers Glenn, I devise a plan. I must go back, back to where my gut is telling me to look. I park my car at the train station, knowing it will be safe and inconspicuous. Walking down the street unshaven, wearing faded brown pants and a forest green jacket, I don't look out of place. Turning onto the main road, I walk swiftly, ducking into the bush when horses or automobiles approach.

Coming to the point of no return, I tighten my belt, then light a cigarette to feed my adrenaline. I nervously scan the surrounding area, then step over the deadfall and slither like a snake, making my way through the woods.

Through the trees and shrubs, the Haggard's shanty is in view. There is no sign of life anywhere, only the stench of rot from the deteriorating buildings. Continuing along the outskirts of the woods, I carefully cross Dickson Creek. A pair of ducks take flight, causing me to panic. I take a few deep breaths, calming my jittery body and tightly grasp the gun in my jacket pocket.

Recalling the trail, I continue through the stand of pines to the protruding rock formations. I stroll toward the open meadow and wait until it's safe to proceed. The bluebells and dandelions rooted in the grassy areas are silent, undisturbed, soaking in the sun. The day's breeze is dormant, adding to the creepiness. My knees weaken the closer I get to the oak tree, which stands alone. Standing over the three sunken graves, I do not remove my hat nor cross myself. Trampled grass around the graves indicates that someone has been through here in the last week.

I take a trail leading down the slope to the spot Orie pointed out and follow it over the mountain. The hair on the back of my neck rises when a raven flies above me, lands on a sycamore tree, and sits there watching me. The urge to have a piss has left me. Taking the Colt out of my pocket, I firmly hold it in my hand while proceeding along the trail.

The trail takes me alongside a canyon wall that reaches above the pines. Like a timeline of a distant past, the stone wall of the canyon has jagged rocks of all sizes and protruding layers upon layers of different colours.

I hear the sound of running water in the distance and continue down the rocky slope. That has to be Dickson Creek. The clear bubbling water rushes downward, twisting and turning, guided by the rocks. Getting on one knee, I set the gun by my side, then scoop water with my hands and drink. Wiping my lips with the back of my hand, I look down and see a reflection in the water of the raven sitting on a rock. Reaching for my gun, I aim at the bird with my finger on the trigger but do not shoot.

Crossing the creek, I make my way upwards onto a rocky ledge at the top of the mountain and look around to get my bearings. The sun is over my left shoulder, so I know that I'm going in a westerly direction.

The Shenandoah Valley flows downward, gracing the landscape as if painted onto a canvas. An outline of a narrow winding trail carved alongside the mountain is within a half-mile. It must be the road Orie was talking about, used during the Civil War to haul the redwood trees. I make my way down the slope toward the road.

The rocky trail soon turns sandy, and small stands of pine trees reach upward. There are footprints in the sand going in the opposite direction. Within a few minutes, I stumble upon a vacant campsite. I switch hands, putting the gun in my left hand. Wiping the sweat from my forehead, I squat, placing one knee on the ground, and listen.

The campfire coals are cold. Old rusty cans that were cut open with a knife are littered everywhere. A makeshift lean-to faces south, made up of a pole tied between two trees and covered over with sticks and branches. Tucked in the corner is a musty, dirt-covered blanket. Cut into the trees is an assortment of carvings and rings. Traced into the sandy soil are weird drawings, and there are rocks placed in circles. The ground is hard-packed within them, looking as though someone has been dancing in the ring. I have heard of satanic rituals in the past and believe I just stumbled upon a cult.

Taking off my hat and wiping my forehead with my arm, I look toward the road. I don't know what I'm feeling or thinking or what the Hell is driving me, but I must go on.

Carefully making my way toward the road, I can see my shadow trembling at my side. Each step is an eternity. My heart pounds, drowning out my hearing. Sweat drips off my forehead into my eyes, and my dry throat craves water. Startled, I look up —my mind cannot comprehend what is before me.

Chapter 34

I reach for a branch on a young red willow tree growing within a clump of dogwoods. My fingers pry off an object that is lodged in a Y-shaped branch of the tree. It's a weathered figure of a doll. It's Aggie, Alice's doll. The same doll Delilah ran off with many years ago.

In a panic, my breath escapes me, and the urgent need to piss takes priority. Tucking the doll under my arm, I quickly unzip my trousers and pee. I look around, sensing I am not alone, feeling as though pins and needles are coursing through my bloodstream. I take a few steps forward. Tied to a naked branch of a sycamore tree is a faded scarlet ribbon swaying back and forth in the breeze. Beneath the tree is a rusty, broken picture frame that once held someone's image from another time. I best get out of here while there is still some daylight. Walking across the narrow road, I break a pine tree branch, allowing it to hang, marking the spot for when or if I come back.

* * *

Climbing to the top of the mountain, I look back to see a serene, calming view. The cliffs and canyon walls are timepieces, layered with nature's paintbrush, displaying an array of colours. Small shrubs circle the pines, seeking protection from the sun during the heat of the day. The trickling creek sends a flow of pure water into the valley below.

I know my eyes are deceiving me, for my gut tells me this is a place of horror, a killing field. Putting the gun in my pocket, I continue on my way while the sun is in my favour.

Staying hidden behind a clump of red willow shrubs, I look into the open meadow. It's all clear, so I quickly walk past the three graves. My skin crawls as if ants are eating me. I begin running through the meadow, past the rock formation, scaring the jeepers out of a doe grazing with her young. Almost pissing myself as they run off, I lean against a tree, letting my heart catch up to the rest of me. Staying to the west side of Dickson Creek, I bypass the Haggard yard site on my way to the main road.

Once again, I duck into the woods when hearing vehicles or horses approaching, waiting until they pass, then continue on my way. The sun has some daylight left before it meets the horizon. I get into my car, but instead of going to the cottage, I turn left when leaving Singers Glenn.

Parking my car behind the inn at Channel Rock, I enter and order coffee and the beef stew. My thoughts are muddled, trying to make sense of what I saw today. The cigarettes and coffee help alleviate the growing tension. This is a police matter. I'm not sure what to do but feel I owe Rebecca something.

I rise with the sun and go to the dining room for coffee, hoping breakfast isn't the leftover beef stew. Luckily, it's ham and eggs. Through the dining room window, I can see the town coming to life. Children are walking to school carrying their books and lunch pails. Following behind a few youngsters are their dogs that congregate on the street near the school.

The police officer stationed in the town walks down the street, heading toward the inn, perhaps for breakfast. I leave some money on the table for my meal and go out the back door to my car. While fueling up the car at the gas station, I get two more packs of cigarettes. There is a hardware store across the street, where I buy an axe and a shovel. Pulling my cap down, I enter the grocery store, asking for a loaf of bread and two cans of Klunk luncheon meat. Setting a six-pack of Coco-Cola on the counter, I take a paper bag and fill it with green gummy sticks.

Leaving Channel Rock, I follow a narrow well-travelled trail, which I believe will take me along the mountainside. Lining the route are redwoods and pines on my left. To my right are cliffs and massive rock formations that protrude to the skyline. Within fifteen minutes, I can see the Shenandoah Valley to my left as the winding road takes me higher into the mountains. The rock cliffs have changed colours the further I go, and the land levels to a plateau that hugs the mountain's edge. Spotting the broken pine tree branch, I stop, putting on the parking brake. Standing on the trail, I'm not sure what to do, but know I must conceal my car. Driving the car four to five hundred feet further, I park it facing the road in a bluff of pines. After chopping down a few small pines to cover the car's windshield, so it will not reflect the sun, I light a smoke and open a cola.

* * *

I look up and see that centuries ago, with the evolution of time, a granite boulder had released from the face of the mountain. It came to rest between two spindly sycamore trees, giving them a purpose and strength as they now tower over the bluff. A sheath of dull, soft moss has entombed the granite boulder, which stands guard at the sycamores' base. Nature's cleansing dew has soaked into the moulded moss, allowing the stone a chance to bleed, leaving a dried reddish trail of scars across the face of the weeping rock.

191

As I get closer, the sycamores, with their twisted and naked branches, take on a ghostly appearance. I crouch down at the base of a tree, allowing my breathing to stabilize. My level of courage requires a pep talk, and I recite the Lord's Prayer in my mind. A raven gracefully circles overhead. Its wings cut through the air effortlessly as it soars higher into the sky.

A breeze sweeps its way through the shrubs. I see something glittering in the distance and grip the gun tighter in my hand, moving closer and closer to the spot. My heart pounds, my eyes go blind, looking into the sun. Within a blink of an eye, I am lying on the ground, spitting sand from my mouth. The gun has fallen out of my hand and lays a foot from me.

I have fallen into a recessed hole. Scrambling to get up, I reach for the gun, then quickly look around, feeling sort of stupid.

I breathe a sigh of relief and brush the sand off my trousers. Standing, I can feel something wet around my ankle. My first thought is: Oh damn! I pissed myself! I look towards my groin area, then bend down, pulling up my pant leg. Blood is dribbling from a cut on my leg onto my sock. Stepping back into the sunken ground, I begin shifting the dirt back and forth with my shoe, then squat down. It's a small human rib cage. I've cut my leg on a child's rib —my blood turns cold.

My mind is overwhelmed. I can't quite comprehend what I am seeing or thinking. Sweat has dried on my skin, and I suddenly feel a chill. My hands tremble as I step back from the makeshift grave.

A raven swoops downward, flying slightly above me. Perhaps it knows what I have discovered. I need to get out of here and regroup my thoughts.

Making my way to the car, I'm continuously looking over my shoulder. I light a cigarette and deeply inhale the smoke as though it is oxygen, then quickly gulp down a cola to revitalize my numb organs.

Common sense is telling me to get the law, for I know this is a burial site. A feeling of eeriness overcomes me. Taking the shovel from the car, I make my way back to the sunken grave. Crossing myself and swallowing several times, I start digging. Sand silts back into the grave while searching, so I begin throwing the dirt further. Soon the shovel makes contact with something. A small skull is exposed. I stumble backward, looking around, horrified at what I've discovered. Leaving the skull where it is, I probe with the shovel, uncovering both arms of the body.

Nervously, I kneel by the corpse. The bones of the arms are together on one side in the grave. Oh, my God! This is someone's dismembered body.

Frantically, I run my hand through the sand, finding pieces of blue fabric. My fingers feel a shoe, and I remove more soil with the shovel, exposing a small pair of leather boots. They were white at one time —the shoelaces remain tied.

Chapter 35

Quickly, I cover up the remains of the corpse with sand from the edge of the grave. Gathering my wits and courage, trying to stay focused, I look around and see more settled places where bodies may be buried. I don't have the nerve or internal strength to waken more of the dead— they suffered enough.

Reality sets in; this is a dumping ground for violated bodies that someone enjoyed murdering. It's impossible to determine how many graves there are or how many mutilated victims. The thought is sickening, but I believe Rebecca is among the dead.

The gun has become a vital part of me, and I hold it tightly in my hand. Continuing forward, the rock circle and makeshift campsite are to my left. The shiny objects are directly ahead, and I slowly walk toward them.

That fuck'n raven! It flies from behind me, knocking my hat off my head with its wing. My body goes into panic mode. Trembling, I step back behind a clump of shrubs. I have a clear shot at the bastard but refrain from shooting, knowing it would alert anyone who may be nearby. The bird stares and cusses at me in a language it thinks I should understand. Its black beak and foul tongue, along with its beady eyes, make me want to strangle it.

I stand in front of the glittering object on the red willow shrub and realize that the raven is a collector of shiny things. It is a grave robber. Perhaps it was trying to keep me away from its treasures.

Shimmering hair bands and ribbons of every colour adorn the red willow. I retrieve the glittering object and begin to cry. In my shaking hand is the heart-shaped necklace I gave Rebecca so many years ago. My fingers caress it as though they are touching her, feeling her soft skin and her last touch.

Uncontrollable tears of sorrow fall to my open palm, soaking the necklace in my torment. I close my mind to thoughts of what may have happened and what ordeal Rebecca suffered. My fingers continue trembling while holding the locket. I ignore my inner voice, telling me not to open it. A stream of tears flows over my heart, which cannot bear the weight and another heartstring breaks. Trembling, I open the locket.

A picture of Rebecca —a picture of me.

* * *

There is no turning back the hands of time or destiny, but I swear to carry out the revenge Rebecca deserves that I promised her.

I know without a shadow of a doubt, it's the Haggards who committed these atrocities. Covering my tracks as well as possible with branches, I make my way back to the car. Planning what to do next, I tuck Alice's doll under the front seat and light a cigarette.

Darkness begins to smother the daylight. The western sky takes charge, retracting the light along with the warmth of the sun. The soft blues of the distant horizon begin to vanish and are replaced with a subtle grey.

Ebony skies usher in the rhythm of the night. Heavy clouds pass over the face of the moon, covering its lonely stare. One by one, the Heavens recall the fading stars, reserving their shine for happier times.

My hand rests on the Colt revolver, which is next to me on the seat. I try to relax, slipping in and out of troubled sleep, constantly replaying images of the horror. Terrifying visions of Edsel and Delilah looking through the car windows haunt me. My wristwatch and wedding band glisten in the sun while hanging from the red willow branches. The recurring dream of sand subtly dropping on my face leaves me feeling helpless. I cannot brush away the sand and try to roll my body back and forth, eventually realizing my arms and legs are severed. They lay next to me in a pool of blood. My dying breath begins to fade. An eerie feeling overcomes me as the last droplets of blood begin to turn cold and leave my body, oozing out of my veins.

* * *

The emerging sun stalls and the backdrop of the horizon begins to turn red, perhaps afraid of the new day coming. Suddenly, it cannot be held back any longer and wedges its way into the eastern sky, giving light to the mountains.

I get out of the car and do a walkabout; nature has left her morning dew behind. It begins to wash clean the leaves of the shrubs and the awaking dandelions that have clumped around the rocks. A rabbit in the distance finds its breakfast as it nibbles on a thistle.

Opening a can of Klunk, I use a screwdriver as a knife and slice off a chunk, drop it on the bread, then force myself to eat. I would bet that the rabbit's thistle is better tasting than this sandwich. The cola does help remove the taste from my mouth. Now I can have a cigarette.

I have one hand in the front pocket of my trousers, holding Rebecca's necklace. The Colt pistol is in my other hand. Walking slowly and carefully upon this desecrated ground, I count 14 spots that could possibly be graves. Most are sunken into the ground, with a clear outline of the grave size and distinct signs where the raven has been picking its loot. Kicking sand with my boot, I cover an exposed rib. Having noticed a few graves have a crest over the resting spot tells me these are more recent burials. I pick up a green button lying on the ground and hold it in my hand as though I am holding someone's soul. Saying a quick prayer, I slip the green button in my pocket, next to the locket.

The raven quietly sits on a branch in the sycamore tree, watching me. Standing my ground, I give it a lengthy stare, making it feel uncomfortable. The nervous bird moves sideways on the branch, then back. Its mouth is open, but for once, it's not screeching at me. Since the bird seems to be squirming, I begin to wonder if the raven knows right from wrong and may have a conscience.

I make my way to the lean-to and squat down on my knees. Pulling out the blanket tucked at the back, I see a partly empty jug of moonshine. There is an assortment of knives lying on the ground, wrapped in a bloody cloth. Half a dozen short ropes lay on the opposite side of the lean-to. The blanket appears to have dried blood and semen stains on it. There are four pegs pounded into the ground. Is this where victims are tied? I do not find any flesh or bone fragments around the area but suspect the raven does the cleaning up. The atrocities committed here are unimaginable. I surrender my thoughts, feeling sick.

Chapter 36

I wake in a cold sweat. My shirt is sticking to my skin and the car seat. Hearing something on the roof, I'm afraid to move. I fumble for my weapon on the floor and cock the Colt pistol, frantically pointing the gun in all directions. All I see is the imaginary ghost-like figures of Edsel and Delilah, reflecting off the windows.

My breathing stabilizes. I place the gun on the seat and wipe the sleep from my eyes on my sleeve, then reach for a cigarette. Before I can strike a match, a thumping on the top of the car scares the bejeebers out of me. Squeezing my legs tightly together, hoping that I don't piss myself, I point the gun at the roof, ready to fire.

Who the fuck is on the roof? What should I do? If I get out, they could jump off the top of the car and stab me. Warily, I envision being cut in pieces and thrown into a sandy shallow grave. My heart rate surpasses the jitters I'm feeling. Chills wrap around my spine, and my hand trembles as I hold the gun. I throw the unlit cigarette, which stuck to my lips, onto the dash and place both hands on the Colt.

Like a cast statue, I am frozen, waiting to fire my weapon. I lose the ability to blink and only see in black and white—the thumping in my chest echoes in my ears. Slowly slumping against the driver's door, I feel the cold steel of the door handle on my back.

Suddenly, without warning, I'm free-falling, painting bloody images of my death within my mind. A constant ringing in my ears prevails. My eyes only see a blur, memories fade, and the will for survival diminishes. Time ceases to exist. Darkness rushes in.

* * *

I hold my aching head, wondering what the Hell happened. Rolling quickly to my right, I pick my gun up off the sandy ground, then stand. There is no one on top of the car. The smell of gunpowder lingers in the air, and I can see a bullet hole in the roof.

Damn it! I must have pulled the trigger when I fell out of the car. It was stupid of me to lean against the door handle with my back. A great detective you would make, I think to myself while brushing the sand and dirt off my clothes.

Looking around, I can't see or hear anyone. Quickly I grab the articles from the roof and sit on the car seat. In my hand is a thin silver necklace twisted around a green hair barrette and a short piece of yellow ribbon.

It must have been the raven on the roof, and these are articles it robbed from the graves. Now I wonder if the bird is sharing with me or perhaps giving me peace offerings. I put the items in the glove compartment and go behind the shrubs to relieve myself.

Getting back in the car, I make myself a Klunk sandwich and force myself to eat. The warm meat tastes rather disgusting, and I wish it were one of my mother's peanut butter and jam sandwiches.

Ugh! I can't force myself to eat it and throw the rank sandwich on the roof for the raven. There are only two colas left in the case. I open one and slide the other under the seat, keeping it out of the sun. Drinking just half the cola, I press the cap back on the bottle, saving it for later. Leaning back in the seat, I close my eyes, hoping my headache goes away.

A thumping sound on top of the car wakes me. I am not alarmed, knowing it's the raven eating my discarded sandwich. The bird pecks at the food as its claws scratch on the metal roof, and I wonder if it is enjoying the Klunk. Suddenly the bird is airborne, soaring high above the car. I watch the raven circle overhead until it disappears. Within fifteen minutes, the bird lands on top of the car again, then quickly flies away. I get out of the car, looking to see if it left anything behind. A shiny 10 cent coin lays on the roof. I put the dime in the glove box with the other items.

The sun gracefully makes its way deeper into the western sky. A cooling trend subtly follows. The air feels heavy, and the hint of impending rain exists. The breeze off the Appalachian Mountains slowly increases in volume, ushering in banks of unsettled grey clouds. Within minutes the sun fades beyond the horizon, and the surroundings slowly cover with a filament of darkness. Passing clouds shroud over the moon's hollow stare— ebony skies soon send cleansing rain to this dishonoured ground.

Putting on my jacket and lighting a cigarette, I make myself comfortable. The half bottle of cola is tempting me, and I cannot control the urge to drink it, wishing there were a few green gummy sticks to munch on as well.

Thoughts of home overtake me, and I wonder how Claudette and Sara are doing. I want to start the car and get the Hell out of here. Let the police deal with this. Then, I think of Rebecca. She deserves retribution. Can I live with myself if I give up my mission now?

The rain passes and settles below, across the Shenandoah Valley. The tops of the clouds are visible as I look through the windshield, down toward the valley. Fog rolls over the area, spreading a sea of churning grey matter. Its ghostly effect holds my attention as it lowers and rises within the valley. A glimmer can be seen in the midst of the churning mass, prompting me to think the Heavens may have opened and sent down a ray of light.

No. Those are headlights coming around the bend in the road. A vehicle's lights shine through the eerie fog as it continues to get closer. The ghostly lights become brighter as they twist up the mountain road.

My heart thumps, then slowly finds its rhythm once more. It's them; it's the Haggard twins. I squeeze the gun in my hand, feeling it give me courage. Even if they drive too far and spot my car, they wouldn't recognize me. It's been years since they last saw me.

It must be the Haggards. I watch the car stop on the trail, then back off the road amongst the shrubs and pines. The headlights go dark, and the engine is shut off. The squeak of a car door is heard in the dark, then another door opens. I can hear voices but can't make out what is being said. Feeling panic within me, I wipe the sweat from my face on my shirt sleeve and hold the pistol tightly. Walking slowly and carefully, I slide my feet along so as not to step on a branch or fall into a sunken grave.

Squatting behind a clump of willows, I hear the trunk of the car close and someone talking. I am within 100 feet of them. A blanket of darkness hangs over the night as the moon is cowardly hiding. My bravery stems from the gun I'm holding. I remain crouching behind the willows, knowing I am safe from them for the moment. Soon the sweat clinging to me turns cold, and I begin to shiver from the chill and fear.

I can hear Edsel and Delilah laughing. Getting on all fours, I crawl closer towards them. Their voices are coming from the campsite. Within a few minutes, a small fire is visible through the shrubs and pines. As the blaze burns brighter, Edsel and Delilah pass a jug back and forth between themselves. From out of nowhere, the raven flies over the two, screeching, and lands on a sycamore branch. Praying the damn bird doesn't notice me, I crawl closer to them, watching them drink.

They begin to take their clothes off. Oh, my God! I don't want to see anymore. I want to get out of here. Then out of the blue, Edsel and Delilah begin dancing within the stone circle. Their hands are raised toward the sky as they dance and chant. They start howling at the moon like wolves. Occasionally they stop to drink from the jug, then move to another circle and continue dancing.

Not wanting to venture closer, I look up at the raven. The bird is content as it continues to watch the pair perform their ritual. Edsel throws more wood on the fire. Delilah stretches her arms upward as if she is praying. She begins chanting in a language I do not understand. Edsel joins in the chant.

I don't know what to do. Should I rush the two at gunpoint and tie them up? Would they attack me, leaving me no choice but to shoot them? How did I ever let things get this far?

The twins drink from the jug again, then lay in the makeshift shelter together. I can't see what they are doing, but from the sounds they are making, I'm sure they are having sex. Delilah repeatedly mutters loud moans with an occasional sigh. I can hear their two bodies connecting back and forth as they fulfill their lusting cravings. Edsel grunts vulgarly, making sounds like a wild boar as they continue fornicating.

After some time, Edsel approaches the fire. He is naked, and his penis remains erect as he throws more wood on the fire. He reaches for the jug and takes a drink, then raises his arms to the sky as if in prayer. Delilah crawls on her knees to Edsel, and begins to fondle his body, then sucks his cock. Edsel continues to chant at the moon as Delilah performs her deed. Eventually, he lowers his hands and places them on her head as she starts stroking his penis. He quickly cums, dispersing his seed onto Delilah's face.

Delilah wipes her face, takes the jug of moonshine and lays on the sand by the fire. Edsel reaches for his pants, removes the jackknife from his trouser pocket, and sits by Delilah. He cuts his palm, then cuts hers. They lick the blood from each other's palm, then paint the remaining blood on their faces.

Delilah gets up and leaves while Edsel sips shine. He stares at the fire, then begins mumbling to the flames as if they are old friends. The flames from the fire respond to him, rising and glowing brighter as he slowly raises his hands.

In the firelight, the outline of his body is enhanced, and I am looking at pure evil. His scraggly, knotted hair has turned partially grey and hangs almost to his shoulders. His eyes have no colour. Delilah's blood that is smeared on his face has dried. He is a scary-looking bastard who resembles a picture that I saw in the Bible many years ago; a caricature of the Devil.

Edsel stands, turning around and around in a circle, chanting loudly. He suddenly stops. He is looking in my direction through the darkness, and I can feel his stare.

Unable to determine where Delilah went, seconds pass slowly. I hear something behind me. The raven takes flight, swooping over me. Is the bird warning me to get the Hell out of here?

Edsel's stare penetrates my mind, and I can feel its slow burn into my empty core— I am powerless.

Where is Delilah? I don't see her.

Chapter 37

Shades of blue— shades of grey weave together, smothering the purples that twist and turn. Images float in and out of my mind, some in black and white, others have no distinct colour. Visions and shadows disrupt any thoughts of who I am or what is happening, or what is to be. A spinning takes me higher and higher as I pass through colourless rainbows and surpass the stars. I'm beyond the Heavens, seeing images I do not comprehend. The hand of the Creator reaches to me. I stretch out my hand but cannot feel His touch and drift endlessly into darkness.

Distant sounds of a choir echo in my ears as they sing 'Amazing Grace.' An orchestra of violinists screech in the background, trying to tune their instruments as the choir continually sings off-key.

Suddenly I am in church, floating above everyone, watching a casket roll in on a bier that has no pallbearers. The irritating sound of a squeaky wheel on the carrier has everyone on edge. Two people from the crowd stand and push the casket to the altar at the front of the church, then remain standing there. Incense rises upward, burning my eyes and infiltrating my lungs. The two standing by the casket open the lid. My blood-soaked arms and legs stain the white satin lining. I'm dressed in the torn and soiled clothes that I wore last. Rebecca's necklace is entwined around my fingers. Through the cloud of incense, the two look down at me. It's Edsel and Delilah.

* * *

My mind slowly wakes, leaving my eyes locked in a scarlet filament of drying blood and dreaded fears. I'm on the ground, cold and unable to move. A pounding in my head persists, reminding me that I am alive. My muscles begin to quiver, feeling the raven's claws dig into my skin as it lands on me. My arms will not move when I try to brush the bird away. I try once more, but in vain, realizing ropes are tying my hands down. The raven begins pecking at my chest with its beak—a hollow sound echoes in my ears. Trying to move, I feel sharp pebbles digging into my back. My legs also are tied to pegs pounded into the ground. Struggling to open my eyes, tears form, wetting my eyelids, and all I can see is a blur. The tears wash away the dried scarlet layer of blood, and my ability to blink returns. There is no sign of Edsel or Delilah.

As my memory returns, the pain in my head worsens. Provoked by its incessant pecking, I loudly yell. "Fuck off, bird! The bird flies away. I listen, hearing the subtle sounds of its wings making contact with the air, then landing on a sycamore branch. The raven is free, unlike me. Staked to the ground, like an animal awaiting the skinning knife —I fear my hide will be taken.

* * *

I must have blacked out for a while, for the sun is retreating in the west. The pain in my head has subsided somewhat. My naked body is chilled to the core and begins to shiver uncontrollably. Turning my head slightly, I see my clothes in a pile about ten feet away from me. Dangling from the pocket of my trousers is Rebecca's necklace. My wallet lays open and personal papers are scattered on the ground. Damn, I wonder where my Colt pistol is?

With the descent of the sun, darkness quickly rushes in. The moon this night is steadfast in its duties, only showing a quarter of itself. The evening winds roll off the peaks of the Appalachians, forcing their way downward, bringing cooler temperatures to the night air. My body no longer shivers, it's numb from the cold, and I'm almost paralyzed.

I breathe quickly, hoping to revitalize my muscles and warm my body. Closing my eyes, I tug on the ropes that bind me with all my might. My efforts are in vain. I'm unable to lift the stakes out of the ground. Struggling with every ounce of strength, I try again, but to no avail.

I'm a dead man, lying here knowing the Haggards will soon carve me into pieces and throw me into a shallow sandy grave. I have no options, not even taking my own life before they get to me. The urge to pee overtakes my thoughts. How do I do it? Just let it go? Trying to ignore the pressure building inside of me, I doggedly pull on the ropes, hoping to dislodge the stakes. The movement makes matters worse, and I must relieve the pressure. Oh, geez! Piss streams from me. I can feel the urine dribbling underneath me, wetting my ass cheeks. Fuck! This is disgusting!

Looking towards the sky, trying to find a solution to getting out of this predicament, I begin counting the stars. Hmm, was that 369 or 379, I ask myself as a falling star streaks across the sky, and I forget to make a wish. Big deal, a lot of good wishing is going to do, but I wish I had a cigarette.

An owl begins to hoot at the moon, or perhaps it is calling its mate, telling it there soon will be fresh meat to pick at. The feeling of being vulnerable and helpless is humiliating and drains the last shred of hope from me.

It must be three or four in the morning. Layers of dew begin to settle on me. I lick my lips, gathering what moisture I can. Not feeling pain, my stiffened body lays on the cold ground like a board. The moon's stare is no longer visible, and the stars lose their glow as a bank of clouds cover the sky. Just as well, star counting is not my forte.

Beneath me, the cold ground trembles as thunder rumbles in the distance. A pair of beady eyes glow in the darkness, staring at me as though I am a snack. Unsure how to keep the animal away, I begin hollering loudly and swaying my bound body back and forth. The devious eyes disappear into the night, but I can hear the animal circling behind me.

A creepy silence grips the night, holding the darkness hostage, adding to my fears and anxieties. The dread of what lurks behind me makes my skin want to crawl away and hide, but it cannot. My mind revolves faster and faster, knowing that I am in danger. Feeling an animal brush against my hair, I hold my breath but do not have to play dead; I think I'm already dead. The thumping of my heart subsides, and the jitters disperse. I cannot think of a prayer to say. All prayers elude me.

I hold my breath and clench my teeth, waiting for the animal's first bite. A stench blends its way into the heavy air, stifling my breathing, causing my eyes to water. It's a fuck'n skunk rubbing its rank tail across my face.

I can't hold my breath any longer and gasp for fresh air. A flush of cold goosebumps covers me. The stinky pest believes it has captured a trophy as it begins to sniff its way around me. My shouting and wiggling do not deter it. Occasionally I can feel its cold nose press against my skin as if it's trying to mark the best spot to sink its teeth into my flesh. Once again, it circles me, but this time it goes between my legs, and I can feel the animal's fur on my thighs. I stretch my neck, watching as it sniffs my groin area, hoping the bastard does not bite. Coughing, forced to breathe the pungent air, I shout every swear word that I know.

Calmly the skunk begins to dig beneath me, where I pissed earlier. From time to time, it stops, turns 360 degrees sniffing the air, then continues digging. The feeling of its fur brushing against me sends my body into a frenzy, and the hair on my body stands directly upward, trying to escape.

The skunk continues to burrow under me, and I can feel the vibration on my ass through the soil as it claws at the ground. The small pile of dirt increases in size, then just as quickly as it began to dig, the uninvited guest quits. I can feel it circling in the hole it dug, then lie down and lick its paws as though it is home. The cold goosebumps have vanished and are instantly replaced with my dripping sweat.

Chapter 38

Time, as I know it, ceases to exist, having no meaning nor sense. There is nothing, just a black empty sky that remorsefully looks down at me. My soul is devoid of any humanity it held. The Haggards have won, severing my self-confidence along with the last of my pride and dignity.

In the midst, the ebony sky breaks, revealing a glimpse of the misty outline of the horizon. The darkness is calm, slowly pushed away, and the night's rhythm is lost as signs of a new day slowly emerge. A horizontal curtain lifts before me, and the awaited sun warms my frigid body.

I start to tremble as the sun revitalizes me. I'm weak and starving. My stinky companion has not left; only occasional shuffling and muffled sounds come from the burrow. Closing my eyes tightly, I visualize writing S O S with the clouds that hover in the sky—telling the world to come and rescue me.

* * *

The endless seconds continually form into columns of minutes. On an imaginary blackboard, I draw a line through the lot, calling it an hour. I don't know if it's keeping me sane or taking me closer to insanity. Judging by the count on my make-believe blackboard of time, it must be close to high noon. The sun swells in the overhead sky, forcing me to keep my eyes closed.

My only friend, the raven, swoops down from the sycamore tree, landing near my legs. It takes a quick look at the resident skunk, crows a few times, then cautiously steps closer to me. The bird flaps its wings, trying to protect itself from the stench in the air, then quickly takes flight.

The skunk exits the burrow, then stops at my feet and looks back at me. I say a few choice words to the pest, hoping it will move on and not return, but it ignores me. It coos and hisses, stepping toward the hole it dug. Three times it revisits the burrow. Each time, she emerges carrying a baby skunk by the scruff of the neck, taking them into the shrubs. I feel somewhat relieved, knowing the odour from the skunk has kept many predators away from me. Despair settles in, and I fear what will happen when Edsel and Delilah return.

* * *

The raven returns, and I begin talking to the bird. As I speak, its dark moss green eyes stare at me, seemingly understanding what I'm saying. Moving my fingers to get the bird's attention, it hops closer to my tied arm. The raven begins to tug with its beak at the knot on my right hand. I continue speaking softly, encouraging the bird to peck at the rope which binds my hand.

Hearing the dreaded sound of a vehicle in the distance, shifting gears as it climbs upward on the switchback road, sends the raven into the skies. I would give anything to join the bird in flight and get the Hell out of here. The sound of gravel beneath the tires gets louder. An overworked engine sputters, then the grinding of gears is heard as the driver downshifts.

My mind is overwhelmed with vivid images and fears as I realize the end is near. My killers are here. A new panic flows in my terrified bloodstream, and wild hallucinations evolve.

The sun has burnt my skin, and whatever sweat remained within my empty core seeps from me, adding to the burn. Naked and staked to the ground is not the way I envisioned leaving this world. Frantically I try to mobilize my fingers to grasp the rope the raven loosened.

The brakes of the automobile squeal as it comes to a stop on the road. Grinding of gears can be heard as the car backs off the trail to its hiding spot. My heart wants to crawl from my chest when a door opens, then another door closes. The squeaky trunk opens, and I can hear the rattling of metal, knowing it is the shovel. Edsel and Delilah are mumbling to each other.

Internal shakes take control. My fingers go numb. My mind goes blank. My eyes remain shut as I cry within myself. The Sunday School prayers, which I memorized so many years ago, have vanished from memory, leaving me unable to recite them as I ask for forgiveness. I am at the mercy of the Haggards.

Clenching my teeth with my eyes tightly closed, I expect a kick or knife in my midsection from one of them. As they kneel beside me, the Haggards are laughing at me, poking me with their fingers. I can smell them— preferring the odour of the skunk.

Forcing my eyelids to remain locked and cemented closed, I draw what may be my last breath. My final view of life will not be that of my killers, and I shut out their voices.

Letting my memories float back to happier times, I smile, thinking of my first crush. The puppy love I felt for Miss Clement, which tickled my mind. I wonder if she knew how I felt about her?

The simple things in life were the best of times, recalling how Rebecca and I would laugh together as we watched the red squirrel scurry around gathering acorns. Oh, and the first kiss Rebecca gave me under the apple tree still warms me.

I focus on Claudette and how she captivated me the first time we met. Her beauty and grace have etched their way into my heart, becoming the lady I dearly love. I smile, thinking of little Sara and the joy she brought into my life.

My thoughts are never far from my little sister, Alice. She may have been a thorn in my side growing up, but I could not imagine life without her. Alice's determination and hard work to become what she wanted to be in life came true. How I wish I could hear her sparkling voice once more.

Mother's heart-warming smiles are never far from my thoughts. She was always there when I needed her, and the love she showed gave me confidence and inspiration.

The whimpers of my best friend, Norma, as I held her in my arms that dreadful night after the Haggards killed her pups. Words cannot express what I felt for her, nor the love she gave me in return.

Then, like the bad dream that I'm living, I recall my Dad's last wish written on his blackboard. Suddenly, my Sunday School prayers all come back to me— but it's too late.

Chapter 39

Feeling a calloused hand slide across my chest onto my thigh, I am startled and quickly shift my body, trying to get away. Without warning, a hand grabs my penis. "Fuck off," I yell, opening my eyes.

Edsel and Delilah stand over me, pointing and laughing. Delilah takes her hand off my penis. She rubs her fingers over my unshaven face and across my lips. Edsel grunts at my reaction and presses his knife against my right nipple. He slowly begins cutting at the base— blood spurts from my nipple.

"Stop, Edsel. Stop!" says Delilah, stammering," as she pushes her brother's hand away, then points and says, "Go, away. He's mine."

From the corner of my eye, I watch Edsel fold his jackknife and leave. Delilah dips her finger in the blood that runs down my rib cage, then tastes it. Rubbing her finger in my blood again, she smears it across my forehead and around my nipples. She pulls a wooden Orange Crush box closer to her and shuffles through it. I see a jug of water and say, "Water, please give me water."

Delilah slides closer to me. She smiles, showing missing and rotted teeth. I can smell her rancid breath on my face as she raises my head and lets me drink from the jug. The water is warm but finds its mark. The rhythm of my breathing increases and saliva returns to my dry mouth. I ask for another drink of water, but she refuses my request, then gets up and walks away.

Time has not been kind to Delilah. Her face looks dry and weathered. Her once red hair is matted and has streaks of lifeless grey running through it. Surprisingly, a red barrette is attached to a straggly clump of hair. Her feet remain shoeless. The thin beige dress she is wearing resembles a used flour sack. It is filthy, and the long sleeves have been used for wiping her nose and face. Blotches of dried blood stain the backside of the dress.

I can hear Delilah and Edsel talking beside the car but can't make out what they say. Upon returning, both look curiously at the pile of dirt and the hole in the ground between my legs. The two jokingly point at the burrow the skunk made and chuckle. Edsel takes the shovel and fills the hole with soil, letting me know he is in control as he whacks my balls a few times with the cutting edge of the shovel. As I shudder, he grins, enjoying the suffering and pain he is inflicting on me.

Edsel kneels beside me, then opens his jackknife and smirks. Saliva bubbles from his twisted mouth and passes through his broken teeth, falling onto my chest. His crossed eyes stare at me, but I am unsure which one is looking at me. His crudely shaven face reveals scars of the past, and I suspect insects may be living in his untended hair.

Firmly he presses the knife against my shoulder, cutting me slowly as I scream. The pain is excruciating as he continues to cut down toward my armpit. I close my eyes and only see red. "Stop, you son of a bitch. Stop." I yell out. Edsel laughs while setting the knife onto the open wound, preparing to cut deeper.

Delilah quickly pushes Edsel away from me, shouting to him, "Mine, he is mine." She stands between Edsel and me, pointing to herself, saying, "Mine."

Edsel seems to be amused by Delilah's reaction and laughs while wiping the knife blade on his pants. He walks to the lean-to, sticks the knife into the ground and sits, then gulps moonshine from a sealer and rolls a cigarette. The welcome smell of the smoke he purposely blows in my direction infiltrates my lungs, soothing internal frustrations. For a split second, my body relaxes, and I forget the predicament that I'm in —I need a cigarette.

Delilah sits beside me and touches my cracked lips with her fingers. Her sweat leaves a stinging sensation. Shifting my head to one side, I glare at her when I feel the irritable touch of her fingers trailing down my chest to my abdomen, circling, then stopping. Suddenly she puts her hand on my testicles and penis, causing me to jolt from side to side. While massaging my cock, she mumbles something I don't understand. Edsel excitedly stands and comes closer, pointing at my unresponsive penis.

"Sit down, Edsel. He is mine," says Delilah to her brother. He calmly picks up the jug of shine, has another drink, then wanders off with the shovel.

My life expectancy no longer is measured in years or days; I am down to the nitty-gritty as the minutes slip away. I must and will do anything to survive this perverted madness. The repulsive thought of being used as a sex toy and then getting cut into pieces eats at my mind, spreading its repugnancy throughout me like an active cancer. I begin to comprehend what their victims went through —the last string which held my heart breaks. Now I know the Hell and torment Rebecca experienced. My only hope is, God granted her my place and share of Heaven.

* * *

The air begins to cool as the sun recalls the warmth it bestowed. The light which shone so bright from the skies vanishes slowly, and only subtle greys remain. Clouds hesitantly enter as if performing a graceful dance in a vast ballroom, intertwining with each other. Eerie gusts of wind echo along the ground where I lay and block out the sounds of what my oppressors are doing and planning.

From nowhere, my friend the raven lands close to my side. I speak softly to the bird and wiggle the fingers of my right hand. The bird does not hesitate and begins pecking at the rope. The heat of the day has loosened the ropes that bind me, and I feel a bit of slack.

The dreaded grey and ebony skies return once more. The sun sets in the valley below, allowing darkness to seep its way in, smothering any daylight from sight. The raven abruptly flies into the night, leaving me alone once more, and the evening tightens its grip.

Hearing the rustling sound of shrubs rubbing against clothing, I know the twins are approaching. They each carry an armful of sticks and branches, dropping the wood by the firepit. Edsel prepares to start a fire while Delilah sits on the ground near me. Reaching into the wooden box, she unwraps a small package. The smell awakens my senses as she tempts my lips with a piece of pork jerky. I open my mouth in hopes that she will feed me. She dips her finger in and out of my mouth a few times, teasing me. Delilah gets excited and giggles to herself before releasing the food. Quickly, I chew the meat, savouring the taste before swallowing. I force myself to smile at her, and she gives me another chunk, then another.

Speaking quietly, so Edsel won't hear, I say thank you to her. Delilah slides her finger across my lips, then puts her finger in her mouth, licking it. I innocently look away— my thin, disguised smile disappears as she fucks me with her eyes.

Chapter 40

Delilah stands, brushes away the sand that sticks to her dress, then straddles me. With the cold stare of the moon in the background, she eagerly raises her dress and lowers herself onto me. Her warm ass cheeks rest on my thighs, and her forest of vaginal hair smothers my penis.

Oh, fuck! I'd rather be dead than do this, runs through my mind. Desperately trying to block out what my cock is feeling, I lay helpless, wishing for this nightmare to end. My terrified eyes watch as she leans toward me. With her open mouth, she kisses me. Her repugnant breath momentarily stops my breathing. My pride and whatever ego I have left flows along with my saliva to the pit of my stomach.

My suffocating penis feels the warmth of her wet pussy moving slowly back and forth. Delilah slides the shoulders of her dress down, allowing her breasts to find freedom. In the light of the gaping moon, I can see a huge dark brown birthmark that runs across one of her tits and up her neck. She rubs her breasts while stroking her clitoris over the head of my cock, moaning to herself. With eyes closed and her head thrown back, she rides my uncooperative body, harder and faster. Her fingernails blindly claw at my rib cage. I can feel her ass cheeks tighten as she gets closer to an orgasm. Tantalizing heat rushes around my genitals as warm drops of her magic flow onto my shaft. Pre-cum involuntarily expels from my cock. I guiltily turn my head.

Delilah unexpectedly leans forward, dropping her nipples onto my bearded face, as she squirts a hot flow of the orgasmic fluids over my cock and balls. Feverishly, without warning, my cock begins rising and hardening —with a heartbeat of its own. She loudly moans, releasing her pleasures once more. I can feel her pussy contracting as she enjoys another orgasm.

Edsel comes to her side, "Delilah, Delilah. My turn. I wanna fuck too."

"Go away," she says, remaining mounted on my cock.

"You said I could fuck too," says Edsel as bubbling saliva runs from his mouth to the ground. His cock is bulging in his pants. He's excited and nudges Delilah to get off me.

Violently she swings her arm at him, "Go away; he's mine."

"My turn," he says. "Then we cut him into pieces, like the others. You promised me a turn."

I hope to Hell he's not thinking what I'm thinking. I wish I had my Colt to shove up his ass and pull the trigger. Delilah is the only one who can save me from the degradation he wants to impose on me. Searching for words that may encourage her to defend me, I force myself to say, "Delilah, I want you. I want you, not him." I no longer fear death— but fear that son of a bitch.

Delilah stands and pushes Edsel back a few feet. "Come, Edsel, let's drink by the fire," she says.

Relieved, I turn my head and watch the pair share a jug of shine. He eventually rolls a cigarette for her. She puffs the smoke deep into her lungs, relaxing her body. Edsel is agitated and frustrated, perhaps jealous of his sister.

Delilah gets up and walks to me with the jug, giving me a drink. The homebrew burns my throat and my empty stomach, but it's a good burn. "Thank you," I say with a smile.

Delilah smiles, then walks back to the fire and her brother. Edsel throws more wood on the fire. They share a few more drinks, then under the watching stars, they shed their clothes and begin dancing within the circle of stones. Their drunken slurs and chanting are not understood. I continue watching the pair as they parade naked, performing their satanic ritual.

Soon, their raised arms lower onto one another. They begin kissing and touching each other. Within the circle of surrounding rocks, Delilah drops to her knees, sucking Edsel's cock. He pumps her mouth with his stiff penis while firmly holding her head.

Edsel pulls his cock away, takes Delilah by the hand and walks her close to me. His cock dangles freely as he tells her to get on all fours. He quickly slides his cock into her vagina, pumping her deep and fast. Perhaps in his simple way, he bids for her attention, proving to me that she likes him more than she likes me. The bastard is jealous of me.

My head turns in the opposite direction, refusing to watch them conduct their sexual act. Hearing the sounds of their fornicating and orgasms does not excite me. They disgust me. Edsel revels in his performance, poking my stomach with his finger, trying to get me to watch. Again, he pokes me. I refuse to watch and face the opposite direction. Frustrated with me, he pulls his cock from Delilah's vagina and angrily begins beating on my abdomen with his fists.

Delilah quickly rises to her feet and grabs Edsel around the neck with her arm, dragging him away from me. She kicks at him, saying, "Mine, he is mine. Get away."

Edsel cowardly gets up off the ground. Wiping the saliva from his face, he stands motionless, glaring at me. I can read his mind —knowing he will kill me tonight.

Chapter 41

Edsel sits by the fire, drinking moonshine and smoking a cigarette. Occasionally he looks in my direction, mumbling to himself. He plays with his jackknife, intentionally raising it toward the light so I can see it, then grins at me as he licks the blade.

Delilah has returned from behind the shrubs, where she relieved herself. She kneels beside me and raises my head, holding it as she gives me a drink of water. "Thank you," I say, smiling at her, hoping she doesn't lift her dress and climb on me again. Delilah returns the smile and runs her fingers over my bearded face. I look up at her, surprised to see tears running down her cheeks. I remain silent.

Perhaps the past has caught up with her, and she feels remorse. Delilah wipes her eyes, leans over and kisses me. Unexpectedly, I feel a tear forming in my eye, but it's not a tear of love. It's a tear of pity. Somehow, I feel sorry for her.

Rising to her feet, Delilah walks over to her brother and has words with him. I can't hear what is being said but know Edsel is getting a scolding. I begin to think that she may be the more dominant of the two and the leader, not the follower. She then walks to the lean-to, and picks up the blanket, then covers me with it. Edsel whines and grunts like a wounded bear, but Delilah ignores him.

* * *

The fire begins to lose its glow, and darkness rules the night. The Heavens have opened, displaying a beauty that words cannot do justice. The Milky Way is sprinkled over the ebony sky, enhancing the luminosity of the stars. I pray for a falling star to grant me a miracle, but my hopes are fruitless, and I fall asleep.

My sleep is constantly interrupted with bouts of extreme anxiety and cold sweats. Edsel is asleep near the firepit as the dying embers begin to fade. Occasionally, I see him twitch. Delilah is sleeping in the lean-to. For the moment, I'm safe and try to find sleep once more but fear the vengeance Edsel may seek tonight.

The hoot of an owl fades as a gentle hush sweeps in, and darkness silences. Edsel crawls toward me with his jackknife in his right hand. On his knees, he looks down at me while throwing the blanket aside. I feel the cold night air rush over my naked body as it becomes exposed to him. The dribbling foam falls from his mouth onto my chest. His sneer widens as he rotates the knife in his hand. There is no time for prayer; this is the end. Closing my eyes —I await my fate.

The knife's cold blade nicks my midsection, and I feel its sharpness against my skin as it slides toward my groin area. His cold hand covers my mouth, preventing me from calling out. He teasingly presses the blade against my penis and scrotum. I desperately try to break the hold of the ropes that bind me. Gasping for air, I manage to bite his palm. He quickly releases his grip, cuffing me across the chin. For a moment, I am stunned.

His filthy hand firmly covers my mouth once more. I can see a gleam in his distorted eyes as he pushes the blade against my throat and begins cutting. Feeling the warmth of blood on my skin as it drips down my neck, I hold my last breath and watch my life pass before me as I float above.

Without warning, a loud gunshot cuts the night air. Then within a heartbeat, another shot. My ears ring, blood splatters onto my face and body. For a second, Edsel remains suspended in mid-air, like a statue. The pressure of the knife eases off my throat, and then his body falls on me. Delilah is standing a few feet away. Both of her hands grip my Colt pistol.

* * *

Delilah drops the gun and buries her face in her hands. She stands there crying, then slowly steps closer to her dead brother and me. My body and mind are in shock. I have no feeling, no emotions, no pain. I'm dumbfounded, and everything is in slow motion.

The blood from Edsel's body is running to my groin and trickles down my ass. Pieces of his brain are lying on my chest; they wriggle like crawling worms as I breathe. My piss is uncontrollable and dribbles from me.

Delilah takes her brother's hand, pulling his body off me and dragging him toward the firepit. Against my shivering skin, I can feel the cold steel blade of the knife, which fell between my armpit and elbows. Working my arm back and forth, I manage to conceal the knife under my arm.

Without speaking, Delilah kneels beside me and wipes the blood from my face with the sleeve of her dress. She then takes the blanket and covers me up. To my surprise, she crawls under the covers and snuggles close to me, sliding her arm across my chest. I lay there, wondering what the Hell is happening.

Delilah is sniffling and crying to herself. Her arm grips my chest tighter, and I feel the warmth of her body against my skin. My body gradually releases the tension of the past hours as the night begins lifting slowly over the mountain tops. The first signs of the sun sneak through the narrow horizon.

I can feel her heart beating faster as her hand slides under the covers, onto my testicles and penis. Nervously, I twinge from side to side as she strokes my limp cock. Delilah burrows under the blanket and begins to suck my cock vigorously. She's ripping my aching heart out along with my conscience. Guilty sadness paints across my mind cloaking the innocence I should feel. Staring at the sky, I refrain from closing my eyes, trying to ignore what is happening.

Delilah pauses briefly, moaning and breathing quickly. She has an orgasm but continues sucking my penis. Her desires have not been fully satiated.

I feel embarrassed; guilt rushes in, compounding my defenceless feelings. As she slides the blanket to the side, Delilah's leg slips over my midsection, and her hands press against my chest. I feel her wetness on the tip of my partially erected penis. She grasps my cock, and forces it into her waiting pussy as her vagina savours every inch of my stiffening cock. I turn my head away as she starts fucking me slowly with long strokes. Her bouncing ass stimulates my testicles the harder she rides me. Her fingertips dig into my skin. She fucks me faster, releasing short bursts of lube around my cock. Delilah begins to moan repetitively, and her tense body relaxes, allowing a flush of her fluids to flow onto my balls. My body responds, and my penis ejaculates; my reluctant mind does not.

Chilled to the bone, I lay on cold, damp ground. My sanity, which I managed to retain, slowly disintegrates. I am a victim of my own making. Fuck the guilt— I survived another day.

Chapter 42

Delilah takes the shovel, walks past Edsel's body and disappears. I suspect she is going to dig a grave for her brother. Damn! It may be for me also. The thought of being thrown into the same grave with Edsel gives me the creeps. Looking around, I can't see the pistol anywhere and bet she has taken it with her.

I was hoping she began to trust me since Edsel's death, but it appears she does not. What are her plans for me? A sex toy, staked to the ground for her sexual gratification? A companion to run wild with through the villages and farms, stealing and killing at random? Without a doubt, she has to kill me, and I can't foresee any alternative end to this madness.

The raven flies toward me from a sycamore branch. The bird must have been reading my mind. It stares at me as though it has something to say. I know what the bird would say, and it may not be kind. I wiggle the fingers on my right hand, beckoning the raven to my tied wrist. Its intelligence surprises me as it pecks and pulls at the rope. My heart thumps, seeing the progress it makes.

Startled, the bird flies away when Delilah approaches without the shovel. Maybe she will untie me to help carry Edsel's body to the gravesite. She stands over me and smiles without saying anything. I bite my tongue and do not speak, only smile as we make eye contact.

Delilah begins dragging her brother's body on the hard-packed ground, over the shrubs and logs. She is crying and talking to herself about the painful task she is coping with. Inside of my empty gut, I can imagine what she feels and sympathize with her.

The raven soon returns. I begin to feel slack in the bindings as the bird manages to pull the rope loose with its beak. Finally, I have a free hand and reach for the knife under my left arm, cutting the rope that ties my left hand. Painfully sitting up, I cut my legs free from their bindings and carefully rise to my feet. I am wobbling, dizzy, trying to keep my balance. Blood rushes through my body as though it has found new routes. A flush of tears flood onto my cheeks. My fingertips tingle, my head pounds.

Slowly taking a few wobbly steps to the water jug in the wooden Orange Crush box, I drink quickly. Scared out of my wits, I look in every direction for Delilah and begin putting on my clothes. Walking feels like a new experience that awakens aches and pains. Movement causes the wound on my neck to reopen, and blood dribbles onto my collar. I cut the bottom off my shirt with the knife and wrap the cloth around my neck to curb the blood flow.

My knee joints feel like they're welded solid, and my arms are stretched beyond their limits. The more I move, the more my body loosens up and revives. I take another drink of water, then quietly begin the search for Delilah.

* * *

Squatting behind a clump of red willows, I watch Delilah pull Edsel's lifeless body into the grave she prepared. Oddly enough, it is located in the centre of the other graves.

Should I make a break for it now and get the police? What if Edsel and Delilah did something to my car, and it won't start? Delilah has my gun, and she knows how to use it.

Thoughts bombard my mind, my arms and legs ache, and the pain in my back is excruciating. Feeling somewhat dizzy, I do not trust my judgment. My gut tells me to get the Hell away from here. I sneak behind the shrubs and rocks in the direction of my car.

I can see my vehicle in the distance and carefully make my way toward it. Quietly opening the door, I get in, but there are no keys. On the seat is the half-eaten can of Klunk, which the flies are now enjoying. The glove compartment contains a road map and a few other useless items. I get out of the car and check under the seat, only seeing Alice's doll. Could the raven have managed to pull the keys from the ignition? Damn! Edsel and Delilah must have discovered the car, and one of them has the keys. Shit! In all likelihood, they're in Edsel's pocket.

I turn to close the car door; Delilah is standing there, pointing the gun at me. "You're mine," she says, raising her hand and pointing. "Go."

Delilah follows close behind me. We stop at Edsel's grave, and she points to the shovel. I pick it up and begin covering his body with soil. Delilah sits a few feet away, crying, wiping the tears on her sleeve. The gun remains gripped tightly in her hand. She may be mourning but keeps a watchful eye on me. While working, I talk to her, trying to comfort her, hoping she relaxes and puts the gun down. She pays me no heed as my words fall on deaf ears.

I throw the last of the dirt on the grave, forming a crest on top. Delilah stands, picks up a stick and walks a few steps. With the stick, she draws a rectangle in the dirt, then steps back, looks at me and says, "Dig. You, dig."

The sun glares in my eyes as I look at her dumbfounded. My knees weaken. Still holding the shovel, my hands begin sweating. Damn it! She wants me to dig my own grave. Without blinking, she stares at me with a cold expression on her face. She aims the gun at my head —I begin to dig.

Throwing dirt to either side until the perimeter is dug, I then step inside to continue digging. Delilah comes closer, watching me work. Sweat drips profusely from my forehead, causing me to wipe my face in my sleeve continually. She hits me across my back with a stick, "Dig."

I turn and look at her, forcing a thin smile from my parched lips. She grips the stick tighter, waving it, trying to intimidate me. Tears run down her cheeks like the waters of Dickson Creek. Feigning sympathy, I reach my hand out to her. She stands motionless, bewildered, not knowing what to do.

Delilah's emotions have caught up with her, and she drops the stick. Her tears vanish as her lost smile struggles to return. The hand holding the gun relaxes slightly while her free hand tempts fate and reaches for mine.

From nowhere, the raven lands, screeching and clawing on Edsel's grave. Delilah is startled and fires the gun at the bird. Instinctively, I hurl the shovel at her, knocking her off balance. The Colt revolver falls from her hand. We wrestle for control of the gun.

In that split second, my life flashes before me as the gun discharges. Then an eerie silence sets in, along with the sensation of trickling blood on my fingers. For what seems like an eternity, time stands still.

Delilah's eyes go blank but remain fixed on me. I stand looking down at her. With my boot, I push her body into the partially dug grave.

My breathing is erratic; my nerves stretched to the limit. I am an emotional wreck. Without hesitation or remorse, I pick up the Colt and pull the trigger again and again —until the gun is empty.

Chapter 43

Delilah is lying in the shallow grave she'd forced me to dig, with blood trickling from her bullet wounds. I drop to my knees next to her. With trembling fingers, I touch her face, somehow not believing she is dead. I close her eyes for the last time. I'm no better than her, knowing neither of us will enter God's sanctum and will be forever — 'The Unforgiven.'

Down deep within my hollow core, my conscience stirs. Feeling I owe Delilah something, I reach into my pocket for Rebecca's necklace. Tears obstruct my vision as; I remove our pictures from the locket. Taking Delilah's hands and placing them on her chest, I intertwine the necklace around her fingers, then remain on my knees and cross myself, praying she is at peace.

Tucking the Colt pistol in my trousers, I pick up the shovel and begin digging up Edsel's body. My gut churns angrily, wishing he was still alive so I could beat his fuck'n head in with my fists, killing the son of a bitch.

Stepping into the partially uncovered grave, I search his cold dead body. My quivering hand slides into his overall pocket, finding five marbles and the keys to my car.

* * *

Driving toward Channel Rock, I turn onto the main road that takes me to the cottage, slowing down while following a team of grey Percheron horses pulling a wagon load of pine logs. After they turn toward Singers Glenn, I continue driving to the lake.

Entering the cabin, I take the pack of cigarettes off the counter and light one, then open a Pepsi and sit on a chair, resting my feet on the table. It feels as though I just came back from another world. My thoughts of the past days rush in, scaring the Hell out of me.

With determination, I walk past the stables to the boathouse, open the doors and look around. After grabbing the gasoline container from the corner and splashing gas on the east wall, I light a match, pause for a moment, then toss it. Within a few seconds, the building is engulfed in flames. Taking a few burning boards from the fire and walking to the stable entrance, I throw the flaming boards inside.

Stopping by the edge of the water and looking down at the spot where I buried the Gummy Stick box with a child's boot inside, I say a prayer, hoping the youngster is at peace. Then, sadly walking towards the graves of the pups, I force a smile knowing their deaths have been avenged.

Once inside the cabin, I shove a Pepsi and the cigarettes in my pockets. Fulfilling my father's last wishes, I set the curtains in the kitchen and dining area on fire, then walk to my car and start the engine. The driveway allows a good view of the roof collapsing in flames. I glance at the lake, remembering some of the good times the family shared, but the pain and sorrow outweigh any of the joy. The magical reflections the waters once held dissipate as though the memories were from another lifetime.

Soon after crossing over the road which goes into Singers Glenn, darkness is rapidly on my heels. I drive carefully on the winding road that takes me to Channel Rock. After looking in the car mirror and combing my hair with my fingers, I walk to the General Store to buy a razor, comb and a new shirt. Then I get a room at the inn and wash up. The beef stew is still on the menu.

The real-life nightmares I experienced invade my dreams, causing me to toss and turn, continually waking in a cold sweat. Butting out another cigarette, I lay in bed, comforted by the thought of seeing Claudette and Sara soon. Hopefully, Mom is alright and keeping busy with her church duties and friends.

Soon the memories of home console me, and I drift off to sleep once more. The good memories quickly fade as the lights dim, and the nightmares project onto a large screen in black and white. I sit, tied to my seat in a movie theatre, watching the atrocities inflicted on the helpless victims. Unable to close my eyes, I yell to Edsel and Delilah, but they ignore my pleas for mercy.

Rebecca looks at me. Raising her arms, she calls my name. My tied hands will not allow me to rescue her, and the Haggards strike her down. I call out to our God to intervene, but He does not. I wake, soaked in sweat, scared as Hell.

* * *

On the road at first light, pledging never to return, I drive, leaving only dust behind. However, the memories follow me like a curse.

The streets of Richmond are alive, with pedestrians on their way to work. The honking of car horns reminds my empty soul that I am home. I smile but soon wipe away a tear while waiting at a stop sign, watching a young boy walking his dog on the sidewalk.

I park my car and walk into Alice's office. "Where in the Hell were you? We've been so worried," she says, rushing into my arms. "So, where were you? What happened?" Alice asks, wiping her eyes in a tissue.

I reach into my pocket and hand Alice her doll, Aggie. She slumps in her chair, shocked, staring at Aggie. "Oh my God, after all these years," she says, looking at me. "Robert, you didn't."

"Um, you best send the police, along with undertakers, to just west of Channel Rock. Dad's last request has been honoured. I am going home."

Turning off the car engine, I watch as a red squirrel gathers acorns underneath the oak tree, then look toward the house and see the curtains move — Sara dashes out the door. Running towards her, I scoop her up and swing her around, then hold her close. Cradling her in my arms, I kiss her cheek then set her down, watching as she runs to her sandbox to play.

Claudette waits in the open doorway. My smile slowly fades the closer I get to her as new fears arise. Our pleading eyes make contact and lock onto each other. Taking Claudette in my arms, our lips meet, rekindling our love.

Uncontrolled tears trickle from my eyes onto her neck. I hold her closer and tighter, not wanting to let her go. Words I've longed to tell her are lost, smothered deep within the disturbing trauma that now haunts me. I kiss her neck, feeling a cold flush of guilt.

"Damn it, Robert. I missed you, and I was so worried. It's good to have you home."

"You don't know how happy I am to see you and Sara. Oh, where did Sara go?" I ask, wiping my eyes.

Claudette walks to the window, sliding the curtain open. "Robert, come here, look at Sara."

I shudder in disbelief. Sara is playing in her sandbox and talking to the raven as though they were old friends. Oh, my God! My family and I have inherited the curse of Eva Smir.

Chapter 44

Claudette only knows what I told her about my trip to Singers Glenn. My answers to her are vague, merely telling her my father's last wish was to burn the cottage and outbuildings to the ground. She chuckled in ridicule when I said Dad suspected a curse plagued the property at the lake.

* * *

The lonely days pass slowly, and the darkness that comes with the night brings a new fear when I join Claudette in bed. My desire for intimacy fades as quickly as the light disappears from the lamp on the nightstand. Laying on my back sends me into a dreadful frenzy, and I promptly turn to curl up on my side. Closing my eyes to find sleep seems fruitless, and I shudder when Claudette's lips and fingertips tease my edgy body. Arousal, along with my sexual appetite, no longer exists. My body has become frigid—fearing the touch of the woman I love.

Delilah's perverted sexual manipulation of me while being tied torments the depths of my soul. The stench of her breath and body remains sourly embedded in my nostrils, at times causing me to swallow continuously to prevent myself from vomiting. Perhaps the shameful, licentious sexual deeds forced on me may have saved my life, yet a haunting exists that is slashing at my heart. How do I explain to my wife what happened?

Frustrated with my inadequacy, Claudette turns to her side of the bed and finds sleep. I quietly get out of bed, slipping my hand under the mattress for the Colt revolver, and sit at the kitchen table sipping bourbon. The ashtray fills with cigarette butts the more I drink. The feel of the gun in my hand feeds my soul, restoring my dignity.

* * *

The first snow fiercely blew in off the Appalachian Mountains the third week of October, blanketing Richmond in two feet of snow. With the sudden snowfall, the trees bared their foliage, and the city became a barren winter land.

With heavy hearts, friends of the family and church members helped carry Mom's casket through the drifted snow to her waiting grave. The church choir sang our mother's favourite hymns, and Alice read the eulogy.

Sadness struck our family again. Soon after our mother's passing, Alice's husband, Cecil, died of a massive heart attack. Then, Alice's son, Arthur, was diagnosed with polio within two weeks of his father's death. Our hearts bled for the youngster, who would never walk again.

The campaign trail was brutal and lonely without Claudette and Sara at my side. A bottle of bourbon kept me company between the whistle stops. I wrote my short speeches on empty cigarette packages. The red, white and blue banner, bearing my name, had been ripped off at our first stop. I told the train conductor not to blow the whistle when we reach Singers Glenn and just pass through the town without stopping.

Shortly after the ballots were counted, I turned the radio off; my ineffective campaign cost me the election. I was out of a job. The voters had spoken. It was painful enough losing my seat and position in the Legislature. But, reading the note that I found under the bourbon bottle the next morning severed my last heartstring, sending my broken heart into the pit of my stomach. Claudette had left me, taking Sara with her. In a moment of despair and rage, I burnt the note.

The house that I lived in mysteriously burned one evening. Homeless, I moved into our mother's house, sharing space with Alice, Peggy and young Arthur. My first thoughts were to blame the raven and the curse for burning the house, but then realized I hadn't seen the bird since Claudette and Sara left.

* * *

Some fifteen years have come and gone. Time has left me bitter. The past has eaten away at my soul, and I feel cold and hollow, much like a bared tree, only giving way to the passing wind.

Alice's daughter, Peggy, married Peter Sims. They bought a house near Highdale School, where they both teach. Young Arthur has been a role model for the family. His determination and strength, living daily with polio, has given him courage. He is now in his second year of university, studying science and medicine. I have become very close to Peggy and Arthur, for I believe they guided me, helping me find peace within myself. I pledged to Alice and myself that I will always be there for them and do whatever is necessary to keep them safe.

After supper, Alice sat beside me and asked me to meet her for lunch the next day at Arnie's, next to the city park. She said there were a few things she wanted to go over with me. I accepted her invitation and met her for lunch.

"Robert, I'm over here," Alice calls out, waving to me to come to the booth where she is sitting.

"Hey, Alice. What's happening?"

"I took the liberty of ordering you a coffee and hamburger steak."

"Great. Thanks, Sis."

"Oh, here's our food. Dig in, Robert."

"So, what is so secretive that we couldn't talk about it in the house last night?" I ask, sliding my empty plate to the side of the table and taking a sip of coffee.

"Well, um. I didn't want Arthur to hear us. It's a very delicate matter, and I'm not sure how to tell you, Robert. Claudette and Sara were murdered in their house in Harrisonburg two weeks ago. The office just got a notification yesterday. I happened to stumble upon the bulletin when it came to the records department."

My voice raises in disbelief, "What the fuck are you talking about? They were murdered?"

"Robert, lower your voice. Let's go talk in the park."

"Alice, I don't understand any of this," I say, lighting a cigarette and sitting down next to her on the park bench. "Explain what you just said."

"Robert, they were both murdered. Sara and Claudette. I talked to Captain Able in Harrisonburg, and he confirmed what I am telling you."

"Oh, my God! I can't believe this. I best get to Harrisonburg and make arrangements. Alice, you better come with me."

"No. It's not necessary. Everything has been taken care of. Claudette may have been your wife, but the two of you were divorced years ago, and Sara was of legal age. The funeral has already taken place. They are buried next to each other in Hamel Cemetery."

Chapter 45

There is no heart remaining in this body of mine to ache. My soul begins to bleed, pouring over memories that are coming alive. I feel the rusty nails of crucifixion slowly pounded into me. How much Hell can a man go through in half a lifetime?

"Robert, there's more."

"More! How can there be more? They're both gone. Claudette and Sara are both dead, and it's all my fault."

"Listen to me. It's not your fault. Um. Shit! I don't know how to tell you this," says Alice as she pulls a few papers from her purse.

Standing, not wanting to hear anymore, I light another cigarette and walk away from the park bench toward the metal railing that runs along the river bank. Blindly, I stare at the water as it flows downstream, wiping the tears from my eyes. Alice approaches and stands close to me, putting her arm around my waist. We both stare at the water in silence.

After a few minutes, we walk back to the bench and sit. We don't speak, just look down at the grass, not seeing anything.

Hesitantly, Alice breaks the silence. "There is no easy way to tell you this, so I'm just going to blurt it out. It's going to hurt. Your deeds to rid Singers Glenn of the Haggards, and uncover the atrocities they committed, was a feat beyond what any man should have to endure. The Police Department and the families are grateful to you, even though you wanted to remain anonymous. I'm especially proud of you, Robert."

"Yeah, so, that was a long time ago. What does that have to do with anything?"

"It seems like a lifetime ago. If you recall, when you came to see me and told me to get the police and undertakers to Channel Rock, I did. The police also went to the Haggard Farm. They found two kids in the shanty, perhaps about four years old at the time. They were twin girls. We presume they were Edsel and Delilah's children."

"Are you serious? How can that be? Alice, you knew this fifteen years ago. Why didn't you tell me then?"

"I didn't think there was any point in telling you then. The twin girls were taken to Harrisonburg and placed in the orphanage. Neither was adopted. When they came of age, they fended for themselves. Both were in and out of Harrisonburg's jails many times. They have a list of crimes longer than my arm, from prostitution to theft and now possibly murder."

"Murder! You're saying that they murdered Claudette and Sara. But why? What are the odds of that?

"When Claudette went to work at the Harrisonburg Gazette, she wrote for the paper. In her articles, she used her married name, Claudette Billings. Somehow, they knew the name Billings. In their minds, they were avenging the death of their mother and father."

"Damn! After burning our cottage, I had a gut feeling I should stop at the Haggard shack and burn it to the ground also, but I just kept driving. I'd had enough and couldn't take any more."

"Robert, the police believe that the twin girls will be coming after us. They won't be stopping at just you and me, but Arthur and Peggy. Oh, Robert, I'm scared!"

"Alice, tell me the truth. Were Claudette and Sara's bodies mutilated?"

"Yes, they were. Both bodies were sexually violated and dismembered," says Alice as she begins crying uncontrollably.

"What are those two little bitches' names?" I ask in a rage.

"It's ironic, but the names given to them are biblical, Martha and Mary. The description reads; both are 5'5'', 105 lbs, long scraggly red hair, grey eyes. Tattoos cover their arms and lower back, and both are apparently, left-handed. According to Captain Able, they're a pair of wildcats and prostitute themselves to get what they want from men."

"Mary and Martha, huh. Yeah, I remember. Delilah was also left-handed."

"Robert, don't even think of going after them. The police will see to it that they are arrested and brought to justice."

* * *

Coyotes always return home after a kill to regroup. I suspect the Haggard girls are no different.

By late afternoon, I have a few sandwiches made, and the car fueled. My heavy jacket and boots are in the back seat. I tuck the Colt revolver into my belt and stash 50 rounds of ammunition in the glove box. The sun has begun to recede in the west, calling the night to cover the road in darkness.

It's almost midnight when I stop for the night at Channel Rock. The innkeeper warms the leftover beef stew and makes a pot of coffee for me. Since I'll be hunting animals, I want to smell like one and pass on having a shower.

At daybreak, I leave my room, grabbing a coffee from downstairs for the road. Children are making their way to school with their faithful dogs walking alongside them. The children are looking forward to life. I'm planning to take lives. Hmm, it would be nice to be young and carefree again.

The fog begins to lift and dissipates into the morning air, leaving a serene calmness. Slowing down while driving into Singers Glenn, I notice a few pickup trucks parked at the old Redson Store. The livery stable is gone, having been replaced by a garage with gas pumps. It looks as though Arnie's gas station may be the hangout spot in the town. Parking my car at the train station parking lot, I walk toward Redson's Store.

Grabbing a Pepsi from the cooler and opening it, I browse through the store. My stomach turns, seeing the cans of Klunk on display. Within a few minutes, the last of the patrons leave, and the storekeeper calls me to the counter.

"Just the Pepsi?" asks the storekeeper.

"No. I'll have a six-pack of Pepsi to go. Um, also a dozen of those bulk wieners in the cooler, and a loaf of rye bread. Oh, and a bag of green gummy sticks."

"Sounds like you're going camping."

"Well, kinda. I'm surveying Dickson Creek. Can you tell me where I can find the Haggard girls? I need their permission to continue my work. Oh, give me a jar of mustard, also."

"Them two," says the storekeeper as he shakes his head. "When Mary and Martha are in town, they hang around the gas station. That's where they pick up extra cash."

"Oh, they work there?"

"No, I mean, they prostitute themselves, flaunting their bodies to passing vehicles. They may be doing a better business than Arnie. They're a damn scary pair."

Chapter 46

Leaving Redson's Store, I look toward the gas station and see a small gathering. Two redheaded females are talking to a couple of guys who are fueling their pickup truck. After paying the attendant for the gasoline, the men get in the vehicle and drive away. The two young women walk back to the gas station's steps and sit on a bench, sharing an Orange Crush, conversing with the service attendant.

The light of the day is slowly slipping away, and greying clouds are forming, sending a chill into the village. Grabbing my heavy jacket and putting on my boots, I lock the car and walk to the road that will take me out of Singers Glenn. To avoid being seen by anyone, I slip into the bushes when passing vehicles approach.

Reaching the Haggard farmyard before nightfall, I find a comfortable spot in the woods where I can see the main road and their dilapidated shanty.

Cold wieners dipped in the mustard jar and wrapped in bread, hmm, not bad at all. Ah, the Pepsi hits the spot.

Eventually, darkness smothers the landscape, and along with the chill in the air, an eeriness prevails. The wind that rustled the fall leaves by day now lies silent. A rabbit scurries through the foliage, stopping from time to time, listening for predators as it makes its way to its burrow. The lonesome sound of a whippoorwill echoes through the forest as it calls to its mate in hopes it soon returns home. A lone coyote howls, cutting the night air as it pays homage to the moon. The wakening moon wraps itself securely in the warmth of passing clouds— a sense of evil lingers this night.

A vehicle travels down the main road with its headlights piercing the darkness. The flickering strobes of light dancing between the trees cause me to panic, and I hide behind an oak tree. Gradually time passes as if it has no fear of the dark. Flipping my jacket collar up, I sit down and lean against the oak, waiting for the Haggard girls to come home.

* * *

Dawn's heartbeat slowly wakens, the horizon begins to unfold, revealing morning's first light. The forest is now visible, as though it was previously trying to hide from the night. The rising sun causes the morning dew to spill off the leaves and plummet silently to the damp ground as shadows replace the dark.

The rabbit that sensed danger during the night continues on its way. A cottonmouth snake, awakened by the rabbit, slithers under the golden-brown layer of leaves seeking a morning meal.

No one came into the farmyard during the night. I am damp and cold from the morning dew and struggle with the moist matches to light a cigarette. Puffing on the smoke while getting up to warm myself, I look up at the oak tree and see a heart shape carved into its trunk. My finger traces the initials; OD and TH. Hmm, Orie Dodge, that old bugger, he was in love with Teress. My blood flows warm for a moment as I smile, thinking of my friend.

To kill time, I walk to Dickson Creek and wash my face, avoiding looking at my reflection in the water. Memories of where the trail took me many years ago flood back to torment me. I return to the oak tree to sit and wait.

Dusk returns, as does the ominous darkness. Butting out my cigarette quickly, I watch as an older Chevy car turns off the main road and into the Haggard's yard. The two redheaded Haggard girls get out of the car, followed by a young man in overalls carrying a jug. They go into the shanty, lighting candles to illuminate the room. Soon the smell of smoke drifts in the air as it funnels through the chimney. Only the moon is staring down at me as I begin creeping carefully towards the cabin, gripping the Colt tighter with each step.

Peeking through the smudged window, I see the twin girls sitting on the bed sharing a cigarette. They are identical in appearance. Both are wearing tight-fitting bluejeans. One of the twins wears a red low-cut sweater, the other a black and white checkered shirt with the top buttons undone. Their jackets and boots litter the floor beside the stove.

The man that followed them into the shanty looks too damn young and innocent to be there. He pulls money from his pocket and gives it to the girl in the checkered shirt. She carefully counts the money and tucks it into her jeans pocket. The nervous lad stands with his jug, takes a swig, then passes it to one of the girls. Soon, the three begin drinking moonshine as though it's water.

Within a short time, one of the twins reaches toward the lad and pulls him closer to the bed. The other girl stands, unbuckling his overalls. He clumsily steps out of his clothing. Standing there naked, he appears to be bewildered and frightened, as if he wants to run home to his mother.

The girl in the red sweater begins running her fingers through his hair and kissing him. The other drops to her knees and starts stroking his hardened penis. His youthful body quivers as she begins to suck his cock. He gasps for air, moaning in delight and pulling on her red hair as he pumps his cock to the rhythm of her sucking mouth.

After a short time, the twin girls stop arousing him and giggle to each other. The lad's cock dangles like a lone willow branch as he begs them to continue. They tease and taunt him until the youngster reaches for his overalls and pulls out more money.

Without further hesitation, the two girls go to their knees. They take turns sucking his throbbing penis as though they are sharing a piece of licorice. It doesn't take long till the lad howls like a young coyote as he releases volleys of potent sperm onto the twins' faces and hair.

Damn it! What the Hell do I do now? I can't just rush in and kill all three. I'm beginning to question whether or not I have the stomach to commit cold-blooded murder.

The girls remove their clothing, giggling to one another—the lad excitedly stares at the naked twins. His cock finds life once more, like a planted corn sprout in a windblown field. He is willing and anxious to explore multiple sins of the flesh.

He lies on his back, tasting the sweetness of one of the girl's nipples as they tease his watering mouth. Her twin sister begins stroking his cock vigorously, then straddles his anticipating body, sliding onto his firm erection. She wildly rides him, leaning back, placing her hands on his legs.

Meanwhile, the other girl removes her nipple from his mouth and kisses him. Whispering to him, she rises to her knees, turns and sets her pussy on the lad's mouth. She slowly twists and turns her quivering buttocks on his face. His sweaty hands squeeze her ass cheeks as though he was rubbing a magical genie and making a wish. The twins then begin kissing and caressing each other as they fornicate with the young man.

The young lad's stamina is quite remarkable. Both girls are on their knees on the bed. He stands barefoot on the floor, going back and forth, servicing both of them, leaving each with a deposit of his seed.

The sexual exploits continue. I step away from the window, not wanting to see any more, and walk behind the cabin while lighting a cigarette. The moaning and squeaky bedspring sounds are loud enough to shake the cobwebs from the outside walls.

Chapter 47

Finally, the young man's desires are sated—he stands, drained from the sexual deeds. He lights a cigarette, and the three drink from the jug as it is passed back and forth. One of the girls runs outside, naked, peeing by the shanty door.

The lad puts on his boots, steps out bare-assed, and goes around the corner of the cabin. He pisses against a tree, grunting to himself as though he is a comic book hero who just saved the world from destruction. Now's my chance.

The barrel of my gun pressed against the back of his neck causes his hair to stand on end as I menacingly say, "Okay, you young bastard, I caught you fucking those girls." Cocking the trigger, I continue threatening, "Get your little prick in the front seat of your car, and drive away while I'm still in a good mood. If you turn around or come here again, I will cut your sack off with a sardine lid and nail your balls to a tree. Is this understood?"

The young fucker is too terrified to speak and only nods as piss runs down his leg and into his boot. I hold the Colt to the back of his head and walk with him to the car, then step back into the darkness as he hurriedly drives away.

Closing the cabin door behind myself, I angrily stand before the Haggards with my gun pointed at them.

"Who the fuck are you! Where's Jimmy? What the Hell do you want?" questions one of the girls as they scramble for their clothes to get dressed.

I fire a warning shot into the floor and menacingly shout, "Sit down on the bed. Now!"

"If you want our money or a piece of ass, just say so, Mister." says the other girl.

"Shut up! You two little tramps killed my wife and daughter," I say, choking on my words.

"Mister, mister. You have that wrong. It wasn't us."

"Are you not Mary and Martha, twin girls born to Delilah Haggard?" I shout at the top of my lungs. The two sit on the edge of the bed, trying to entice me with their thinly disguised smiles.

The colt revolver I hold begins to have a heartbeat of its own, and I feel the sweat from my trigger finger run into my sleeve. I clench my teeth, searching my soul for courage. In the blink of an eye, I shoot, then shoot again. Both girls fall to the floor —dead.

Walking back into the forest, I turn and watch the flames engulfing the burning shanty light the night sky. Unexpectedly, from out of nowhere, the raven lands on a branch of the oak tree. Silently, its beady eyes stare at me. Friend or foe? I walk away without saying a word and make my way to the main road.

I am delirious. My eyes water with a purple mist falling from the sky, showering me in guilt. The moon retracts its glow and hides its view within the clouds. The stars this night soon are covered over by God's hand, perhaps fearing to shine on me, wary that I may have become the cursed.

* * *

A quiet hush falls over the courtroom; the Judge drops the gavel on the desk. The Hangman's noose tightens around my neck. Time splits the night. Each second becomes more painful, as though I'm burning in a Hell of Heaven's discarded stardust. Voices of whispering Angels gradually fade into obscurity. The rusty nails of crucifixion release their hold. Freefalling into a darkened silence— I feel the touch of Rebecca's hand.

Manufactured by Amazon.ca
Acheson, AB

11151852R00155